CAPTIVE

E.D.G. SMITH

CHAPTER 1

THE BADGER GANG STRIKES

Wednesday, 19 October 1880: The team of six horses leaned into their collars as they pulled the stage up the hill. The horses kept their pace as the road narrowed and went between a large boulder and a tree. When the stage reached the narrowest point there was a thump on the roof of the stage, causing the passengers to look up.

"What was that, Pa?" asked Audrey Benton.

"I don't know."

"Whoa," shouted the stage driver as he pulled back on the reins, bringing the stage to a stop.

Masked men on horseback carrying rifles surrounded the stage.

"It's a holdup," said Audrey's brother, Brad; "just like before."

"Don't say anything or make any sudden movements," warned Harold Benton, their father. "Do exactly what they tell you to do. Don't argue with them."

Audrey thought to herself, *this can't be another holdup. When we rode the stage in May, the Big Foot Gang held up the stage. Am I jinxed? Every time I ride the stage, there's a holdup?*

"Everyone, out of the stage, now!" commanded a heavyset man waving a rifle at the stage door.

Brad slowly opened the stage door, climbed down, and then helped the three elderly passengers down the steps. Audrey came down next followed by their father.

"Go behind the stage and look down the hill," commanded the heavyset man, pointing with his rifle.

Everyone walked behind the stage and looked down the hill as ordered.

"Sit down, now!" he ordered.

Everyone sat down in the road. Brad and Audrey helped an elderly lady sit down.

The man turned to the stage driver and said, "Throw down the strongbox, and no sudden moves."

Jim Bates did as ordered. He slowly reached down, pulled up the strongbox, and then tossed it to the ground. He was a little over six feet tall with a medium build. Jim had been the stage driver for several years and his blue eyes contrasted nicely with his short black hair. He looked at the man with the rifle, obviously the leader of the gang. He knew that the Overland Stage rule was to cooperate during a holdup. The lives and well-being of the passengers and drivers were more valuable than a strongbox. Jim watched a small man dismount and pick up the strongbox.

The small man carried the strongbox to the side of the road. "This box is mighty light, Boss," he said, dropping it on the ground.

"Use your rifle and open it," said the boss.

The small man stood back from the box, aimed his rifle, and fired a shot at the lock, shattering it. Reaching down, he lifted the lid, "It's empty!" he exclaimed as he showed the box to his boss.

"Get down from that stage," yelled the boss, waving his rifle. Jim Bates climbed down keeping his hands high.

The boss got off his horse and climbed into the driver's seat. Turning to Jim he screamed, "Where's the gold?"

"That's the strongbox I was given this morning. They never tell me what's in it."

Cursing, the boss picked up the shotgun that had been tossed to the ground and fired both barrels into the side of the stage door. A large hole appeared in the center of the door. Grabbing the barrel of the shotgun, he smashed it on the right front wheel of the stage; the stock of the shotgun flew off the road.

"Everyone, back into the stage," he shouted throwing the barrel of the shotgun in the direction of the broken stock.

Brad and Audrey helped the elderly lady up from the ground and into the stage. While they helped an older couple climb aboard, Jim Bates climbed back up into the driver's seat. The wife of the couple kept shushing her hard-of-hearing husband as Audrey boarded. Brad climbed into the stage. Just as his father was about to follow, the boss stopped him.

Motioning at Harold Benton, he said, "You, git over here."

Their father stepped down and went to where the boss had pointed.

"No gold, so we're taking a passenger," laughed the boss.

The small outlaw rode up beside Harold Benton, and taking his left foot out of the stirrup said, "Behind me."

Harold put his foot in the empty stirrup and swung up behind the man.

"Before we head out, I've got a message for the stage company," said the boss, pulling out his six-shooter. He pointed the pistol at the driver and fired.

"I just winged ya'," said the boss. "Next time have some gold for Duke."

The boss rode to the front of his men, "Head out." The outlaws took Brad and Audrey's father and galloped up the road and around the bend.

CHAPTER 2

BRAD DRIVES THE STAGECOACH

When the rumble of the horses' hooves had faded, Brad said, "They've shot Mr. Bates. We'd better check on him."

"Pa did everything they asked," cried his sister. "Why did they take him?"

"Because Duke Badger is an evil man," replied Brad. "I read about him and his gang in the *Denver Post* that Pa had in his office."

Brad and Audrey jumped out of the stage, rushed to the front, and looked up at Jim, who was pale with shock. "How badly are you hurt?" Brad asked as he climbed into the driver's seat.

"I'm bleeding pretty bad." Jim grimaced while he held his shoulder.

"Audrey, check those trees for some moss," said Brad. "We've got to stop the bleeding."

Brad pulled his kerchief out and pressed it against the bleeding wound. Audrey gathered some moss from a nearby tree and ran back to the stage.

"Here's the moss, Brad," she said fighting back her tears as she climbed up to them.

Brad had already removed the driver's shirt. He

pressed the moss against the wound and covered it with his kerchief.

"Audrey, I need some strips of cloth. Open Pa's bag and tear up one of his shirts. We'll wrap it around Mr. Bates' chest to keep the moss and kerchief pressed against the bullet hole."

Audrey grabbed her father's bag from the top of the stage, opened it, and removed a shirt. "Brad, I need your knife."

"Here," he said, handing her his pocketknife.

Audrey cut the edge of the shirt and began tearing it into strips. Then she tied the strips together to make them long enough to go around him. While pressing the moss and kerchief against the bleeding wound, Brad and Audrey wrapped the strips of cloth around the driver to hold the bandage tight. In a few minutes, the bandaging was complete.

"Mr. Bates, tell me how to turn the stage around so we can go back to Riverton," said Brad.

"Keep going up the hill. There's a spot about a quarter-mile ahead where we can turn around. Since we're going up a hill, take the reins and slap them once. These are good horses; they'll start pulling. As soon as they do, you release the brake. If you release it before they start pulling, the stage will roll backwards. Then the team would have to stop the backward roll of the stage before they can start pulling it forward."

Brad slapped the reins, the horses started pulling, and he released the brake. "It worked!" he exclaimed. "I'm driving the stage."

"The turn-around is just ahead." Jim pointed with his good arm. "Slowly pull back on the reins till the horses are walking. That's good. Now gently pull the reins to the right until we're well off the road. Good. Now to the left, and we'll circle around and head back down the hill toward Riverton. There's a way station a few miles back where can stop for help."

Audrey looked at the driver. His eyes were closed and his face was pale. "We'll be at the station in a little bit," she said encouragingly.

Audrey had her left arm behind the Mr. Bates and held onto the baggage rail. Her right hand gripped his right arm, helping him to sit up as he gave instructions to Brad.

"I see the way station," said Brad. "I'll pull back on the reins and press the brake with my foot."

"Don't press the brake too hard," he said. "It's okay to let the horses walk a little."

Brad walked the team to the front of the way station and then stopped the stage.

"Jim!" exclaimed Brennan O'Neil, running to the stage. "You're hurt! Let's get you inside and check you out. What happened?"

As they helped him down, Audrey told Mr. O'Neil about the holdup and why the driver was shot.

"That must have been Duke Badger. Your father told me about his gang."

"It was," said Brad. "One of his men called him Duke. Pa had a copy of the *Denver Post* in his office which had a story about him."

Mrs. O'Neil cleared a table and rolled a blanket to put under Jim's head. Brad and Mr. O'Neil helped Jim lie down on the table.

"Good bandaging," said Mrs. O'Neil removing the bandage. "Who did it?"

"Brad did," said Audrey as she nodded toward her brother. "He's good at it. He bandaged my arm this summer. Mrs. Adams told me that he'd done a good job."

"Well done," said Mrs. O'Neil.

"Thanks," said Brad. "Can you help him?"

"I'm not a doctor, Brad. You've done what I could do. If this was an emergency, I could probe for the bullet. However, Doc Adams is only four hours away. I'll do some more wrapping for the stage ride, but you should take him to Doc Adams. He can remove the slug and fix him up right. Let's get him back on the stage so you can get going to Riverton."

"Brad's a pretty good driver," said Mr. Bates. "He handles the team well, so I think we'll manage."

"Well, since he's a good driver, you're helping him, and I've only got one arm," said Brennan O'Neil, "there's no need for me to come along."

"Let's get you back on the stage and to Doc Adams," said Brad.

"Here's a canteen of water, Jim," said Mrs. O'Neil, "and here's some laudanum for the pain if you need it."

Brad helped Mr. Bates back into the driver's seat. The three elderly passengers agreed to ride with Brad driving, so Brennan O'Neil helped them re-board the stage.

Audrey climbed up into the seat beside Brad and Jim Bates. "The passengers are in, and the doors are closed, even the door with the hole. Let's go."

Brad released the brake and slapped the reins. The horses immediately started forward.

"Let 'em set the pace," Mr. Bates instructed. "They're an experienced team. The lead horse sets the pace, and the others follow. When you approach a sharp turn or a steep hill, pull back on the reins a little, and they'll slow down."

The jarring ride of the stage caused him to grimace in pain. After about fifteen minutes, he pulled out the bottle of laudanum, put it to his lips, and took a swallow.

"The pain's getting worse?" asked Brad.

"Yes, but I can only take little of this stuff. If I take too much, I'll fall asleep. Then I won't be able to help you."

"As soon as we get back, we'll send a wire to the Denver office," said Brad.

"What are we going to do about Pa?" asked Audrey. "We've got to help find him!"

"I'm worried too," said Brad. "Mr. Bates' wound is still bleeding, and riding on this stage aggravates it. Pa taught us how to bandage, but we're not doctors."

"Both of you are doing fine," he said. "Your father would be right proud of you if he knew what you're doing. You've probably saved my life with your bandaging, and there's no way I could drive this stage alone."

"Thanks, Mr. Bates," said Audrey.

"I'm starting to get a feel for the team and stage," said Brad, "but I'm really worried about Pa. I know Audrey is, too."

"Your Pa's a smart man. He's come out of bad situations before, and he'll come out of this one too."

"I want to believe that," said Audrey, "but I'm still afraid. Duke Badger's a nasty, mean, and evil man."

"Yes, he is an evil man," replied Jim. "But your

father's a remarkable man. He's told me some real hair-raisers about the Civil War; they make this look like a church social."

"Pa told you about his battles in the Civil War?" questioned Brad.

"He fought in the war, same as other men, like Jake Jackson and Tom Shadden."

"But Tom was in the Confederate Army," said Audrey. "Pa was in the Union."

"True," he replied, "but there's a bond between soldiers, even when they fight on different sides, especially after a war."

"Pa was in worse situations than this?" asked Brad. "He's just been taken captive by a gang of outlaws."

"And the leader, Duke Badger, is an evil monster," said Audrey.

"Your father knows how to handle himself, and it looks like he's done a fine job preparing you for life as well. He takes you to church and sends you to school. He and Running Bear have taught both of you about the outdoors."

Brad thought about how Running Bear had trained them how to track and his recent teaming with them in the capture of the Big Foot gang.

"So this is kind of like a test," concluded Audrey.

"I don't mind tests at school," said Brad, "but I don't like tests that involve other people's lives."

Brad gently pulled back on the reins as the stage started down a hill. He looked at the trees and rocks and thought about his father. *Sheriff Tate won't be able to start searching for Pat until tomorrow morning.*

By the time the posse reaches the holdup site, it will be noon.

Suddenly the right front wheel of the stage hit a hole in the road. The wounded driver groaned from the painful jolt and uncorked the bottle of laudanum to take another swallow of the painkiller.

"There's the stream where we watered the horses this morning," said Brad. "I'll stop and rest the horses."

Audrey looked at Jim Bates and said, "You're getting mighty pale. You should ride inside."

Brad pulled back on the reins, and the horses slowed to a walk as they approached the shallow stream. After their two-hour run from the way station, they were ready for a rest and some water.

"I am feeling a might poorly. My head's spinning and I'm cold. I'd better get into the coach now, while I'm conscious and have the strength to walk."

Brad and Audrey helped him down from the driver's box and onto the floor of the stage. Audrey put her carpetbag under his head as a cushion.

"I know you don't feel like it, but you need to drink some water," said Audrey.

"We'll be in Riverton in a couple of hours," said Brad. "Mrs. Jones can hold your laudanum and canteen."

"I'll watch him real close, young feller. You just drive this stage so we can get him to a doctor," said Mrs. Jones.

"Come on Audrey, I may need your help," said her brother.

Brad and Audrey got back on the driver's bench. Brad released the brake, slapped the reins once, and the horses quickly returned to their previous pace.

"Brad, I'm scared. What if we never see Pa again? What if Mr. Bates dies?" said Audrey.

"I'm scared too! Pa is in the hands of that evil man, but," Brad paused, "we mustn't let Duke Badger decide what's going to happen. We have to take charge. Reverend Wesley calls Duke Badger an evil monster, and now we know why. I don't know how, but we've got to save Mr. Bates and find Pa. We can't let Duke Badger win."

"Brad, I've never heard you sound so angry," said Audrey.

Brad gave his sister a puzzled look, thought for a moment, and replied, "I guess you're right; I am angry. Right now, we're doing everything we can for Mr. Bates. Let's think about how we can find Pa."

"I'd like to talk to Reverend Wesley and find out more about Duke Badger," said Audrey. "Sheriff Tate talked as if the reverend had met Duke at one time."

"Yes, let's talk to Reverend Wesley and Zeke, who was a member of the Big Foot Gang. Sheriff Tate told us about Zeke being on the work detail with Lutz Hall of the Badger Gang."

"It was some of Duke's gang that freed Lutz from the work detail," said Audrey.

"Before we go to bed tonight, come to my room so we can talk about Pa, Running Bear, and the holdup," said her brother.

"You think what Pa and Running Bear have taught us will help?" asked Audrey.

"Yes."

They rode in silence, thinking about what had happened and what they might do about it. A few minutes later, Audrey looked at Brad and said, "I'm going to ask how Mr. Bates is doing."

Audrey tightly gripped the baggage rail on top of the coach, hit the roof, and shouted, "How is Mr. Bates?"

"I gave him some more laudanum," replied Mrs. Jones. "He's pretty pale, but we're praying for him. You tell that young feller up there to keep driving. We're going to come out of this holdup fit as a fiddle."

The shadows of the trees got longer as the sun descended in the western sky. It was late afternoon, and the pace of the horses was slower by the time they reached the outskirts of Riverton.

"Riverton's only about a mile away," said Brad. "Remember, he's going to recover and Pa's going to come home."

"We're not going to let that...that evil monster ruin our lives," spat Audrey. "We're going to make Ma, Pa, and Running Bear proud of us."

"You bet," agreed Brad. "We're going to get our Pa back."

Brad pulled back ever so slightly on the reins and the horses slowed as they entered Riverton. As they approached the doctor's office, Brad pulled back harder on the reins and shouted "Whoa." Then he stepped on the brake, stopping the stage in front of Doc Adams' office. Sheriff Tate came out of his office next door and looked up to see Brad and Audrey in the driver's seat.

"Mr. Bates is inside; he's been shot!" exclaimed Audrey, seeing the sheriff.

"And Pa's been taken captive by the Badger Gang," added Brad.

"I'll go tell Doc Adams that we're bringing Mr. Bates up," said Audrey as she climbed down from the stage.

"Brad," ordered the sheriff, "get a couple of men to help me move Jim."

"Right away," replied Brad.

The sheriff opened the shattered stage door, saw Jim on the floor, and said, "Jim, can you hear me?"

"Yes," he groaned.

"This is Sheriff Tate. You're in Riverton and we're going to take you in to Doc Adams. Brad's getting a couple of men to help move you. He'll be back in just a minute."

Christopher Schmitt and Hans Finster came running up to the stage.

"Brad told us what happened," said Christopher. "Hans and I can help you. I brought a stretcher that I just finished making for the doctor."

"We can certainly use that," said the sheriff. "Christopher, you and Hans stay here. Brad and I'll go to the other side of the stage."

They placed stretcher beside Jim, and Sheriff Tate and Brad slid him onto it. Hans and Christopher then pulled the stretcher slowly out of the stage. Brad and Sheriff Tate each took a handle, and the four of them carried Jim up the steps into the doctor's office.

"Audrey, what in tarnation are you doin' on that stage?" asked Jake Jackson.

"I'm getting the baggage down, Mr. Jackson. Will you please help me? Brad and Sheriff Tate have just taken Mr. Bates to the doctor's office." Audrey told Jake about the holdup, Mr. Bates being shot, and her father being taken by the Badger Gang.

"Just throw those bags to me an I'll stack 'em," he said. "Then I'll get the bags from the boot."

While Jake Jackson got the bags from the baggage boot, Audrey gave them to their owners. When the baggage was all handed out, Jake came around and looked at the door to the stage.

"Them double barrels really make a hole," he said, poking his head through the hole in the door. "I'll take the stage to the corral. Tell the sheriff I'm taking care of the horses."

Jake climbed into the driver's seat, slapped the reins, and headed off. Audrey placed Brad's, her father's, and her own bags inside the sheriff's office. Then she climbed the steps to the doctor's office.

"The slug was pretty deep, and he lost a lot of blood," said the doctor. "Let's put him on the bed in the other room; I'll stay with him tonight."

The men picked up the stretcher, carried Jim into the other room, and gently placed him on the bed. Rosemary, Doc Adams' wife, tucked some blankets around Jim as the men left the room and closed the door.

"I didn't want to say this while he could hear me," said the doctor, "but I don't think he's going to make it. He's lost a lot of blood, and he's still in shock. Rosemary will bring him some soup in awhile. If we can get him to eat something and keep him warm, and the Lord is willing, he might live."

They heard the sound of someone climbing the stairs. Doc Adams stopped talking, and everyone looked at the door as Reverend Wesley entered the doctor's office.

"I just heard about Jim," said the reverend. "How is he, Doc?"

Doc Adams told the reverend about Jim's condition and then said, "He needs your help now, Reverend. I've done everything I can."

Reverend Wesley opened the door to the back room and entered.

Mrs. Adams sat in a chair beside the bed, holding Jim's right hand. "I'll be back in a while with some soup, Jim. Reverend Wesley is here to see you." She left the room, and Reverend Wesley sat down beside Jim.

Several minutes later, Brad, Audrey, and the others looked up as the reverend gently closed the door to the back room. "Ladies, men, let us bow our heads," said Reverend Wesley. "Lord, Jim's been hurt, and he needs your help. He was shot by Duke Badger, an evil man."

The sound of a horse pulling a buckboard came through the open window. The reverend continued, ending his prayer with, "Jim is a good man. We need him; you need him in our never-ending war with evil. We ask you to please spare his life and let him continue serving you in Riverton. This we ask in the name of your son, Jesus Christ. Amen."

Audrey wiped a tear from her face as Brad put his arm around her. "We've got to send a telegram to Denver," he said to her quietly.

Reverend Wesley looked around and said, "Let's go home and keep Jim Bates and Harold Benton in our thoughts. Pray for them tonight and every night."

"We'll see you Sunday," said Sheriff Tate leaving the room.

"See you Sunday," said Hans Finster, following Christopher Schmitt and the sheriff out the door.

Brad and Audrey went down the steps and saw Jake

Jackson standing beside a buckboard. "I thought you young'uns' could use a ride home," he said.

"We sure could," said Brad. "Can we stop by the depot first? We need to send a telegram to Denver."

"Sure," Jake replied. "Don't worry about your bags; I already got 'em from the sheriff's office. Hop on, and we'll head over to the depot."

"Thanks," said Brad.

Brad and Audrey climbed on the buckboard, and Mr. Jackson headed to the depot.

"Real shame 'bout your Pa," he said. "Sheriff Tate's gittin' a posse together first thing in the mornin'; Duke Badger's just plain nasty."

"When the strongbox didn't have any gold, he took Mr. Bates' shotgun and blew a hole in the door. Then he smashed the shotgun on the wheel of the stage," said Audrey.

"He's got a temper all right," replied Jake. "Here's the depot. Who ya' sendin' the wire to?"

"The Overland Stage office in Denver," replied Brad. "Let's go, Audrey."

Brad and Audrey entered the telegraph office and were greeted by Mr. Donatelli. "Good afternoon, Mr. Donatelli. We need to send a telegram to Denver," announced Brad.

Mr. Donatelli's dark hair, dark eyes, and olive skin showed his Italian heritage. He and his wife, Gina, had come to Riverton ten years earlier. They had two children; Arturo was in the fourth grade, and Enrico was in the third grade.

"Sure, Brad. Is it for your father?"

"Well, it's for the business," said Brad. He explained about the holdup and his father being taken captive.

"I'm sorry about your father. I'll charge it to the Overland account. I'm sure the outlaws dropped him off after a few miles. He's probably made it to the way station by now," said Mr. Donatelli.

Brad and Audrey wrote the message:

Wednesday, 20 October, stage robbed one mile north of Riverton way station. STOP. Driver Jim Bates shot, may not live. STOP. Harold Benton taken captive by Badger Gang. STOP. Brad Benton drove stage with wounded driver back to Riverton. STOP. Brad and Audrey Benton sending. STOP.

"Here's the message, Mr. Donatelli," said Brad. "We've got to go now; Mr. Jackson is driving us home. We'll come back tomorrow."

Brad put his arm around his sister as they rode the buckboard home. Tears ran down Audrey's face, and Brad had a lump in his throat when they stopped under the oak tree in their front yard.

"You've had a tough day," said Jake Jackson. "Let's git ya' inside and tell your Ma and Grandma about the holdup."

Hearing the buckboard, Mrs. Benton and their grandmother, Victoria, came to the front door.

"Brad! Audrey!" exclaimed their mother. "What are you doing back here?"

"There was a holdup north of the Riverton way station. Duke Badger shot Mr. Bates and took Pa," explained Brad as he and Audrey jumped from the buckboard and rushed to their mother. "Mr. Bates is at Doc Adam's office; he may not live."

Abby Benton hugged her children. "Thank you for bringing my children home, Jake," she said fighting back tears. Victoria put her arm around Abby.

Jake tipped his hat and said, "Least I could do, Mrs. Benton. Your husband would be right proud of Brad and Audrey. They bandaged Jim; saved his life. Brad drove the stage all the way back ta' Riverton. They just sent a wire to Denver 'bout the holdup."

"Ma," cried Audrey, "we did everything Duke Badger told us to do, but he still shot Mr. Bates and took Pa!"

"We got Mr. Bates bandaged up," continued Brad, his voice quivering. "He taught me how to drive the stage, but then we had to put him inside before he passed out."

"If ya' need anything Mrs. Benton, just holler, and I'll come help ya'," offered Jake.

"We will," said Victoria, "and thank you."

"Someone's coming," said Brad, pointing to a rider heading toward the house.

"It's Sheriff Tate," said Abby.

The sheriff halted his horse by the buckboard, dismounted, and walked over to the Bentons.

"Evening, Richard," said Abby.

"Evening, Abby," replied Sheriff Tate, tipping his hat. "I came to tell you that fifteen men have volunteered for the posse. We'll be leaving first thing in the morning. I wired Sheriff Strong in Denver and asked him to notify the Army. If they have the manpower, they'll send a patrol to help search for your Harold."

"Thank you Richard; I know you'll do your best," said Abby.

"I thought you should know that Brad and Audrey

did a first-rate job of bandaging Jim. Doc Adams said he couldn't have done better." Sheriff Tate lowered his eyes and coughed.

"You've got something else to say, Richard," observed Victoria. "Go ahead and say it."

"Well, Doc Adams said Jim is pretty bad. He's not sure he'll live through the night. Brad, Audrey, you did everything you could for him. You should be proud."

"We'll pray for him," said Victoria.

"Good night, Richard. Thanks for stopping by," said Abby Benton.

"I'll ride back to town with ya'," offered Jake.

"See you when we come back," said Sheriff Tate. "Good night Abby, Victoria, Audrey, Brad."

The sheriff mounted his horse and headed back to town at a trot. Jake slapped the reins and followed him in the buckboard.

"Ready to talk?" asked Audrey.

Brad looked at his sister standing in the doorway to his room and nodded. Audrey entered and closed the door. Brad sat on the floor leaning back against his bed, and Audrey plopped down across from him, her back against the wall.

"Remember when we went camping with Pa just before school started?" asked Brad.

"Of course, how could I forget? You shot your new rifle, and we had roast pheasant, baked potatoes, and lemonade for supper. Pa helped us polish our shooting skills; we blasted all those pinecones on that old log.

He even taught us how to make a shelter, just in case we're ever in a situation where we need one."

"That was a good pheasant dinner," said Brad. "Your pancakes the next morning were great, too."

"Pa said they sure could have used pancakes like mine when he was in the army," she replied, a smile coming to her face.

Brad gazed out his bedroom window at the last rays of sunshine glinting off the barn. Audrey pulled her knees up, wrapped her arms around them, and looked at her brother. Brad slowly turned his head from the window and back to his sister a moment before speaking.

"If Sheriff Tate doesn't find Pa, will you go with me to hunt for him?" he asked, leaning forward.

Audrey closed her eyes, silently pondering his question. His question was like a distant bolt of lightning. Brad waited patiently for his sister's response. She finally opened her eyes and answered softly, like a muffled clap of thunder replying to her brother's lightning bolt.

"Yes," she whispered, barely audible whisper. "Yes, I'll go with you."

"I knew you would, but I had to ask," he said, slumping back against his bed. "Mr. Bates said that this is one of life's tests. Pa and Running Bear have taught us everything we need to know. We can both shoot accurately, and we know how to ride. Ebony and Blaze are good horses. We know how to cook, how to treat wounds, and how to build a shelter. We even know how to live off the land if necessary."

"Harvest vacation wasn't supposed to be like this," said Audrey. "They closed the school for two weeks so the children could help harvest the crops. Just think what might have happened if we had stayed to help with the harvest instead of going to Denver with Pa. I was hoping to get some music for Ma."

"And I was supposed to get some things for Nana," said Brad.

"We won't get to do those things this year," said Audrey.

"No," replied her brother, "but I'm glad Ma is teaching that class at Riverton Bible College during the vacation," said Brad.

"Yes," agreed his sister. "Thank goodness she wasn't on the stage. I still have the list of things to get in Denver," she said, pulling it out of her pocket.

Brad touched his shirt pocket. "I have my list too."

"Sheriff Tate and the posse should be back by Saturday," said Audrey. "Let's get some sleep; we've got to talk to Reverend Wesley tomorrow."

"Sure," said Brad, standing up and opening the door for his sister. "See you in the morning."

"Good night, Brad," said Audrey. "And thank you for asking me to help you. If you hadn't, I would have asked you to join me in hunting for Pa!"

CHAPTER 3

LEARNING MORE ABOUT DUKE BADGER

Thursday, 20 October 1880: "Audrey, it's time to get up," said Brad as he gently shook his sister.

Audrey rolled over, looked at her brother, and squinted at the sunlight coming through the window. "What time is it?"

"About eight o'clock. Ma's already eaten and left to teach her class."

"What do you want to do?" asked Audrey.

"I think we should talk to Reverend Wesley and Zeke this morning."

"That's right. If we're going to think like Duke Badger, we've got to learn everything we can about him. I know Zeke and Lutz Hall were in prison together. Some of the Badger Gang freed Lutz Hall, who then beat the guards during his escape. Zeke refused to join them. He helped the injured guards into the wagon and drove them back to the prison."

"His act of compassion got the rest of his sentence commuted," said Brad. "Helping those in need helped Zeke."

"He was acting like a good citizen," said Audrey. "He wasn't expecting anything in return."

"I think we ought to see Reverend Wesley first, then Zeke," said Brad. "What do you think?"

"Let's eat first. I'm so hungry I could eat the hooves right off a horse!" said Audrey.

"That's my saying," laughed her brother.

"And it's a good one," she replied with a smile. "That's why I used it."

"Come down to the kitchen when your dressed," said Brad.

A few minutes later, Audrey joined Brad and their grandmother in the kitchen. "Good morning, Nana," she said as she wrapped her arms around her grandmother. "Thanks for letting me sleep."

"Yesterday was a tough day," Victoria remarked, hugging Audrey and Brad. "You both needed the rest. I'll make some pancakes and then we'll decide what we're going to do."

"What *we're* going to do?" questioned Brad.

"Just because I'm an old woman doesn't mean I can't help you plan the search for your Pa."

"How did you know we were thinking about that?" asked Audrey.

"I know both of you. You've cried your eyes out about your Pa. You're not ones to whine and wait for someone else to do your work. Right now, you're angry and you want to do something. I can't stop you. I can, however, listen to you and give advice; how about it? Talk to me while I'm making the pancakes."

"Wellll," drawled Brad, "we're planning on seeing Reverend Wesley this morning. He tangled with Duke Badger several years ago."

"Then we're going to the Bar-X to see Zeke because

knows about the Badger Gang. His sentence was commuted last week, and now he's working for Hank Lacy," said Audrey.

"We want to learn as much as we can about Duke Badger," explained Brad.

"You have to be able to think like that despicable monster in order to understand him," said Nana.

"Goodness," said Audrey. "I've never heard you talk about someone like that before."

"I've met his kind before," she said. "There's nothing nice to be said about him. Duke Badger is a monster, a beast. Make no mistake about it. He enjoys hurting people, so call him what he is - a despicable monster."

"Reverend Wesley calls him an evil monster," said Brad.

"Well, the reverend is right. And don't you forget it."

"We won't," said Audrey.

"Here's the first batch of pancakes. Start eating while I cook up the next batch."

"These are good," commented Brad. "They're better than usual. What did you do differently?"

"I added love for my hurt grandchildren," replied their grandmother.

Brad and Audrey finished breakfast and told Nana about the holdup and the drive back to Riverton. This time, they told her some of the details they had skipped the previous night. When they finished, Audrey started to pick up the dishes to take them to the wash basin.

"I'll do the dishes," said their grandmother. "You two saddle up and go see the reverend and Zeke. Learn all you can about that Duke Badger. We'll talk when you get back."

Brad went to the tack room for the saddles; Blaze and Ebony nickered and came over to be saddled.

"I'll put on the bridles," said his sister.

"Here's the one for Blaze," said Brad handing her a bridle.

They both worked quickly, and in a few minutes, Ebony and Blaze were ready to ride. The horses headed to the corral gate and waited restlessly for Brad open it.

"They certainly want to go for a ride," said Audrey.

"They'll get a good run out to the Bar-X." Brad opened the gate. "First, let's stop by Doc Adams' office. We need to see how Mr. Bates is doing."

Audrey mounted Blaze and waited for Brad to close the gate. As soon as Brad was ready, the horses broke into a gallop and headed down the lane to the Riverton Road. In a few minutes, they arrived at Doc Adams' office. They dismounted and ran up the steps.

"Hello, Mrs. Adams," said Brad as he entered the office. "Is Mr. Bates -," Brad choked and looked at Mrs. Adams expectantly.

"Jim ate some chicken soup last night," assured Mrs. Adams. "He's resting right now, but he asked to see both of you. Please go on in."

Brad and Audrey quietly entered the room. Jim was in bed, wrapped in blankets with his eyes closed.

"Good morning, Mr. Bates. This is Audrey Benton. Can you hear me?"

Jim slowly opened his eyes. "Yes," he said as a smile filled his face. "Thanks for coming to see me."

"You look a lot better than you did last night," remarked Brad. "Doc Adams did a good job."

28

"I heard Reverend Wesley praying for me last night. I told myself I had to live. I couldn't let Duke Badger win."

"We're going to see Reverend Wesley now," said Brad. "He met Duke Badger several years ago. We think he might be able to tell us something about him."

"He's a mean one all right," said Jim. "He went plumb loco when he found the strongbox didn't have any gold in it."

"Ohhh," moaned Jim grimacing as he moved. "I need you to send a telegram to Denver reporting the holdup."

"We did that last night," said Audrey.

"Good," he sighed. "Then George Scott will be sending a temporary manager and an extra driver. They probably left Denver this morning."

"I didn't think about this morning's stage," said Brad.

"Jake Jackson took this morning's stage. Your Pa's had him trained as an emergency replacement for years. Looks like his planning paid off."

"Jim, that's enough talking for now," said Mrs. Adams. "You close your eyes and rest. I'll be back in a little bit with some more soup."

"Bye, Mr. Bates," said Audrey. "Keep eating Mrs. Adam's chicken soup. We're going to see the reverend."

Brad and Audrey left Doc Adams' office and mounted their horses. They talked about Mr. Bates' improvement and their chat with Nana on the way to the parsonage.

"I knew Nana was smart," said Audrey, shaking her head, "but I didn't know she could read our minds."

"I didn't either," said Brad. "It's nice to know that she'll help us."

When they reached the parsonage, they dismounted and looped the reins over the hitching rail. Brad opened the white picket fence gate, and they went down the stone walk and up the two steps to the front porch. Audrey knocked on the door.

"Good morning, Brad, Audrey," greeted the reverend as he held the door open. "I've been expecting you."

"Expecting us?" asked Audrey.

"Yes," replied the reverend. "I figured you two might come by to find out more about Duke Badger. I stopped by and saw Jim this morning. He's doing much better. If you two haven't seen him yet, please do so. He asked to see you."

"We just visited him," said Brad. "After hearing your prayer last night, he said he had to live. He couldn't let Duke Badger win."

Referend Wesley opened the door to the parlor and the three of them entered. The reverend had a seat in his favorite stuffed chair while Brad and Audrey perched on two straight-back wooden chairs.

Reverend Wesley smiled and said, "Jim's going to be just fine. He should be up and around in about a week. In a few weeks or so he'll be driving the stage again."

"He asked us to telegraph the Denver office and report about the holdup," said Audrey. "We let him know we did that last night. He seemed relieved."

"That's good." The smile left the reverend's face as he said, "Now about your Pa. I won't mislead you. Duke Badger is a mean man; there's no way of knowing what he'll do."

"That's why we're here." Brad sat up a little straighter in his chair. "You met Duke Badger several years ago. Can you tell us any more about him?"

"As I said, he's a mean man. I call him an evil

monster. I helped capture him six years ago when I was a deputy in Denver. That was before I went to seminary. The sheriff, five other men, and I met Duke and his partner coming out of a bank they had just robbed. Duke's gun jammed, but that didn't stop him. He threw his pistol at us, hollered, and attacked the sheriff with his bare hands. The sheriff slammed him in the abdomen with a rifle butt, knocking him down. Duke acted like a man possessed; he cursed and tried to fight the seven of us, but we overpowered him. I got some rope from a cowboy and tied Duke's hands behind his back. He kept cursing and started kicking, so I tied his feet, and the sheriff gagged him. We threw him over the cowboy's horse and took him to jail."

Brad nodded. "When Duke discovered the strongbox didn't have any gold, Mr. Bates said he went plumb loco. What makes a man crazy like that?"

"I don't know," answered the reverend. "Maybe as a child he discovered that if he hollered and fought when he didn't get his way, his parents would give in. Or, maybe he made a pact with the devil. I'm sure the Lord knows, but he hasn't told me."

"Is he afraid of anything?" asked Audrey.

"Not that I know of," said the reverend. "Duke Badger is fearless. I don't think he's afraid of anything, not even death. I can usually find something good about a man, even a man who has killed and robbed. But I have never found, or heard, anything good about Duke Badger."

"Does he drink, smoke, like a particular food, or anything unusual?" asked Brad.

"You ask questions just like a Pinkerton," said the

reverend with a smile. "He drinks, but he's not a drunk. I don't think he smokes or chews tobacco. He likes pork and bear meat, but that's just about everything I know about him."

"Thanks for sharing it with us," said Brad.

"Where are you off to now?" asked the reverend.

"We're going to the Bar-X," said Audrey.

"And I bet you're going to talk to Zeke," said Reverend Wesley.

Brad smiled, "How did you know that?"

"I went to see your Ma this morning; then I had a chat with your Grandma. We talked about the holdup, your father, Jim, and you two. I'm glad you listen to your grandmother. She's a smart lady, and she loves you, just as much as your parents do." The reverend stood up. "Be sure and pray for your father; I am."

"We are. Thanks again for your time, Reverend," said Audrey.

Brad and Audrey returned to their horses and trotted slowly through Riverton. Once they were outside of town, they let the horses lengthen their stride for a comfortable lope to the Bar-X.

It was late morning when they reached the Bar-X, and the chill in the air had vanished. They stopped at the foreman's house and looped their reins over the hitching rail.

"It looks just like it did last month when Hank helped us with our roping," said Audrey as they looked at the corral.

"Except there's not any cattle here today," noted Brad.

"I was amazed when you roped your calf and tied it for branding," recalled his sister.

"You roped your calf, too," said Brad.

"But you had to flip it over for me," she said as they climbed the steps to the front porch.

"That's only because you roped such a big calf," laughed her brother. "Your roping was good; the calf was just too big for you."

"I hope Hank Lacy is here and not out on the range," said Audrey as Brad knocked on the door.

Dooley walked up behind them and said, "No one's there."

Brad and Audrey turned around. "Where's Mr. Lacy?" asked Audrey.

"He's due back shortly," replied Dooley. He's fixing Zeke up with some horses."

"That might be them now," said Brad pointing to two distant riders with a small remuda.

"I reckon it's them," agreed Dooley. "They'll be coming directly to the bunkhouse. You might as well ride over there and wait for them."

"Thanks, Dooley," said Audrey. "We'll do that."

A few minutes later, Hank Lacy and Zeke herded the horses into the corral, dismounted, and walked to the bunkhouse.

"What brings you out here?" asked Hank.

When Brad and Audrey told them all about what had happened, Hank and Zeke shook their heads in amazement.

"I'm sorry to hear about your Pa," said Hank. "Sheriff Tate is good. He'll find your Pa. Duke Badger probably dropped him off someplace."

"We hope that's true," said Brad, "but if it's not, we'd

like to learn more about Lutz Hall and Duke Badger. We thought Zeke could tell us something about them."

"Sure," Hank nodded at Zeke, "we've just been talking about him."

"Lutz kept to himself," recalled Zeke, putting his thumbs in his front pants pockets. "But, just before he escaped, he told some tales about Duke Badger. They did some holdups and a little rustling together. Lutz said that Duke had a real bad temper. Duke told him about being captured in Denver; although Duke's gun jammed, it took the sheriff and six deputies to get him into jail. Lutz said if he'd had seven men pointing guns at him, he would have put his hands up and done everything the sheriff told him to do. Duke, however, fought the seven men with his bare hands. Duke's a crazy one all right."

"Did he tell you anything else about Duke? Does he like a particular gun? Is he afraid of something, like snakes?" asked Brad.

"Well, he did say that Duke is partial to bear meat, even though years ago a bear just about killed him. Since then, he steers clear of cliff overhangs and caves. It seems he shot a bear that went into a cave. He looked in, saw the bear, and thought it was dead. However, when he went into the cave to bring it out, the attacked him. Duke emptied his six-shooter into it. The bear knocked Duke on his back, and then fell on him, dead. The bear's head was right in his face, the jaws open. Since that time, Duke's been afraid of caves or any place that looks like a bear would live or hibernate."

"I'd be afraid of caves too if a bear had almost eaten me," agreed Audrey.

"Well, that's about all I can tell you about Duke Badger and Lutz Hall," said Zeke.

"We appreciate that," said Brad. "Are you coming to church Sunday?"

"If Mr. Lacy lets me," replied Zeke looking at his boss.

"You can go to church just about every Sunday," said Mr. Lacy. "We have to have some men available all the time, but we arrange it so all the men can get into town once a week. The exception is during the roundup and snowstorms; then we need all the hands."

"Then I'll be at church Sunday," said Zeke.

Brad and Audrey mounted their horses, reined them toward Riverton, and clucked them to a lope.

"Just about all we've learned is that he's mean, crazy, likes pork and bear, and is afraid of caves," reflected Audrey as the horses loped toward Riverton. "Did I leave anything out?"

"I don't think so. Let's go straight home. I'm hungry."

"I'm hungry too," teased his sister, "so you must be starving!"

"So, what did you learn about Duke Badger?" asked their grandmother as she ladled some venison stew into Brad and Audrey's bowls.

"He likes pork and bear," said Brad.

"And he's afraid of caves," added Audrey.

"Reverend Wesley said he's crazy, and not afraid of anything," said Brad.

"And, Duke Badger likes to hurt people. He'd rather hurt them than kill them," said Audrey. "He likes to see people suffer."

"Did the reverend tell you we met early this morning?"

"Yes," replied Brad, "but Audrey and I don't understand how you and the reverend knew what we were thinking. How do you do it?"

"I was young once, and I've raised children of my own. The reverend learned to figure out what people are thinking when he was a deputy, and even more so as a man of the cloth."

"So you know what we're thinking the same way that Brad and I know what the younger kids in Sunday school are thinking," said Audrey.

"That's it. You out-tracked the sheriff with the Big Foot Gang. If Sheriff Tate's search is unsuccessful, I expect you'll try to find your Pa. If I were younger, I'd be champing at the bit to go with you, but I guess you'll have to go without me.

"We'd take Running Bear with us, but he won't be back from St. Louis for another week," said Brad.

"I know. Now, let's talk about what you're going to do and not going to do."

"We need to stay together," said Brad.

"We'll take Pa's horse and boots, and a complete set of his clothes," added Audrey. "He was only wearing street shoes."

"And camping gear," said Brad.

"I'll get some paper and make a list," said Audrey.

For the next hour, Brad and Audrey went back and forth about what should be on the list. When they were done, Audrey copied it on to a clean sheet of paper. Clothes, food, ax, shovel, hatchet, blankets, frying pan, coffeepot for tea, plates, forks, spoon, and the list went on and on.

"We'll have to buy some things," said Brad.

"We can withdraw some of the Big Foot Gang reward money from the bank," suggested Audrey.

"Now, do you know what not to do?" asked their grandmother.

"We don't want to meet up with the Badger Gang. But, if they have Pa, we do want to free him," said Brad.

"Duke is arrogant and fearless; he'll probably make some mistakes. We'll track him as if we were Running Bear. We'll think like we're Duke Badger; and we'll avoid him," said Audrey. "He won't even know we're there."

"Ten, twenty, even thirty, years ago, pioneer children your age were getting married, building their sod huts, and starting farms. You're certainly old enough to hunt for your father," said their grandmother.

"Duke Badger is crazy, but he wants money. He's too lazy to work; that's why he robs banks and stagecoaches. We'll avoid him," said Brad. "We won't try to capture the Badger Gang."

"I know you won't. Don't even let him know you're around. You'll have to do everything that Running Bear taught you. See, but not be seen. Hear, but not be heard. Track, but not be trackable."

"How do you know all of that," asked Brad as he looked questioningly at his grandmother.

"My husband, your mother's father, was a scout for General Grant. He told me how an Indian had trained them. They were to see, but not be seen; hear, but not be heard; and track, but not be trackable."

"Running Bear can do that, and we can do that. But I don't know anyone else in Riverton that can do that," said Brad.

"That's why only the two of you should go. You can't risk taking an untrained person with you. I talked with Reverend Wesley about that this morning and we both agree; only the two of you should go."

"Nana's right, Audrey, we had best go to the bank now, before it closes," said Brad.

Brad pushed his chair back, stood up, went to the kitchen, and put on his hat and coat. Audrey was right behind him as she put on her hat and coat and followed him out the door. Brad closed the back door, and the two of them silently walked to the corral. Blaze and Ebony waited for them at the corral gate.

The ride to Riverton was quiet, and the horses automatically slowed to a walk when they entered the town. Brad and Audrey gently reined their horses to the hitching rail in front of the bank.

"According to the bank's clock it's ten minutes before three," said Audrey as she dismounted.

"That gives us ten minutes to withdraw some money," said Brad.

They entered the bank and headed to the teller's cage. The afternoon sun reflected off the gold lettering above the teller's cage, momentarily blinding them. Several customers were in the bank, one of whom was Mr. Bevins. Brad and Audrey waited for him to finish his transaction.

"Good afternoon, Mr. Bevins," said Brad. "We'll be over to your store as soon as we finish here."

"Wilma Sue was asking about you," said Mr. Bevins. "Sorry about your father. I'm sure Sheriff Tate and the posse will do their best."

"We know they will," said Audrey.

"I must be going," said Mr. Bevins. "I have a customer waiting. I'll see you in a few minutes."

"Brad, Audrey," said Mr. Nachman coming up to them. "I was shocked to hear about your father being taken captive."

"Thank you for your concern," said Audrey.

"It's almost three o'clock and we don't want to delay your closing, Mr. Nachman," said Brad. "We need to withdraw fifty dollars, what with Pa gone and all."

"I understand," he said. "I'll take care of it personally."

Mr. Nachman went behind the teller cage, pulled out the ledger card for their account, and brought it to the counter.

"I'll need both of you to sign here indicating that you withdrew fifty dollars," he said.

Brad signed the card, and then Audrey. While they were signing, Mr. Nachman got the money from his cash drawer.

"Here you go," he said. "Two double eagles and an eagle."

"Thank you," said Audrey putting the gold pieces in her pocket.

"I see the guard is getting ready to lock the bank," said Brad as they headed for the door. "Thanks again, Mr. Nachman."

"Now to the general store," he said, watching the guard lock the bank door behind them.

A minute later they entered the general store. Mary Sue was handing change to man they hadn't seen before. He turned and headed for the door, nodding and touching the brim of his hat as he passed Audrey.

"I expect you have a list for me. What can I get for you today?" asked Wilma Sue.

"Yes, here it is," said Audrey.

"I'm sorry about your Pa," Wilma Sue said as she started gathering the items on the list. "Sheriff Tate and the posse will do a thorough job of searching for him."

"We know," said Brad, "but we're still worried."

"Duke Badger is a mean monster," said Audrey. "He shot Mr. Bates and took Pa just because the strongbox was empty."

"Reverend Wesley told me a little about Duke Badger," said Wilma Sue. "He is a mean one all right." Wilma Sue looked at the list, and then continued. "Excuse me. I'll have to go to the back room for the kerosene."

Brad looked at the stack of items on the counter and said, "A hatchet, six cans of beans, two slabs of bacon, a..."

Wilma Sue came out of the back room, interrupting Brad. "Here's the kerosene," she said. "That completes your order. Let me total it."

Brad and Audrey put the items in their saddlebags while Wilma Sue totaled the order. Brad looked at the wall clock; it was a quarter to four.

"You order comes to $29.95," said Wilma Sue. "Shall I put that on your account, or are paying cash?"

"Cash," replied Audrey smiling, handing her two double eagles. We just made a withdrawal at the bank.

"Ten dollars and five cents is your change," said Wilma Sue, handing the coins to Audrey. "When is the sheriff due back?"

"He told us Saturday afternoon, at the latest," said Brad.

"We've got to be going," said Audrey. "We've got some chores to do for Nana."

"See you Sunday," said Wilma Sue.

"Sunday," replied Audrey as they left the store.

Brad looked his sister for a moment before he spoke. "You were rather concise with Wilma Sue. You're usually more talkative. Is Pa the reason?"

Audrey was silent for a moment, and then said, "Now that I think about it, I was rather short with her. Pa must be the reason."

They tied the saddlebags to their saddles, mounted, and then headed to the livery.

"Good afternoon, Mr. Donovan," said Brad as they dismounted. "We came for Pa's horse."

"I've been expecting you," he said. "Sorry about your Pa. Here's his saddle, and here's the bridle. I'll be right back with Ginger, that's what your Pa calls her."

"He keeps a clean livery," said Audrey as Alex went to the corral with a rope.

"Pa says -," Brad paused, took a deep breath, swallowed, and then continued, "Pa says it's one of the best."

Brad and Audrey silently stared at the corral as Alex put a rope around the neck of their father's horse. Their father stabled his horse at the livery most of the time, preferring the one-mile walk to and from work.

"Here she is," said Alex, looping the rope over the rail. "I gave her a scoop of oats this morning."

"Thanks," said Brad, placing a saddle blanket on Ginger's back."

"Your Pa paid through the month," Alex said, taking

the bridle from Audrey. "I'll credit the ledger showing that you took the horse today."

He quickly buckled the bridle and cinched the saddle. Then he handed the reins to Audrey. "Your Pa is a good man; he helped me out a few times. I owe him. If you need anything, just let me know."

"We will," said Brad as he mounted Ebony.

Audrey handed Ginger's reins to Brad and then mounted Blaze. Brad clucked, and Ebony left the livery at a fast walk. Audrey was on his left with Ginger between them. When they reached the edge of town, Brad said, "We should load the horses tomorrow like we will if we have to search for Pa."

"Everything should fit," said Audrey. "We're traveling light."

"I know," said Brad. "But, if we have a problem, or find we need something else, we'll have a couple of days to fix it rather than a few minutes on Sunday morning."

After they turned down the lane to their house, Audrey looked at her brother, furled her brow, and said, "I told Wilma Sue we'd see her in church Sunday. If we go searching for Pa, we'll be leaving early Sunday morning. Did I lie to Wilma Sue?"

"I hope not," said Brad. "I hope not."

CHAPTER 4

PREPARING FOR THE WORST

Friday, 22 October 1880: Brad and Audrey finished their breakfast and headed to the barn. Along the wall in the tack room, the supplies were lined up in three sections, one for each horse.

"I'll saddle the horses," said Brad feeling the apples in his jacket pocket. He opened the door from the tack room to the barn, and put his right hand into his jacket pocket. Ebony immediately came to him and nuzzled his right arm. "Good girl. Here's your apple."

Blaze was right behind Ebony and stamped her foot. "I have one for you, too," assured Brad, offering her an apple.

Ginger walked up beside Blaze and nickered. "No, I didn't forget you." Brad offered his father's horse the last apple.

Brad quickly saddled his father's horse and then Blaze. Audrey finished bridling the horses and watched her brother swing the saddle onto Ebony's back in one fluid motion.

"You've really grown over the summer," said Audrey. "You put the saddle on so effortlessly."

"Chopping wood helps," said Brad, tightening the

cinch. "Now let's load the horses. I'll put the tarp on Pa's horse."

Brad put the tarp behind the saddle and tied it down, then the saddlebags, the shovel and the axe. Audrey put her saddlebags on Blaze and tied her blankets behind the saddle.

"Now for Ebony," said Brad, tying his blankets behind his saddle. "Wrapping the blankets in our old slickers will keep them dry if it rains or snows."

"It will probably snow," said Audrey. "I put a pair of snow glasses in each of the saddlebags, including Pa's. They're the ones Bear taught us how to make last summer."

"We still have six sacks of food and oats for the horses," said Brad stroking his chin thoughtfully. "That will be two small ones for each of our horses, and the two large ones for Pa's horse. In a few days, we'll be down to the sacks on Pa's horse."

"Now to walk the horses around the corral," said Audrey. "That will be the first test."

Audrey led Blaze out of the barn; the other horses followed her. Brad and Audrey mounted and took a couple of laps around the corral.

"No problems that I can see," said Brad. "Let's ride them down to the creek, at a good trot, and see how the loads ride."

Brad handed Audrey the reins to Ginger and opened the corral gate. Audrey left the corral and waited for her brother. Brad mounted Ebony and left, leaving the gate open for their return.

"Ready?" asked Audrey looking at her brother. Brad nodded, and Audrey clucked Blaze to a comfortable trot and headed to the creek. Brad brought Ebony up to Audrey's right, with their father's horse between them. When they reached the creek, Brad reined to a halt.

"Let me retie the tarp," said Brad. "I didn't tie it down tight enough." Brad dismounted and adjusted the tarp before checking the rest of the load on their father's horse.

"Check Ebony, too," said Audrey, dismounting and removing the saddlebags. "I heard some clinking."

"I heard it too," said Brad, shaking his saddlebags. "Mine are quiet. Are yours the noisy ones?"

"Yes," said Audrey looking inside one of her bags. "The butcher knife was rattling on a tin mug. I'll get an old flour sack and wrap the mugs when we get home."

Brad mounted Ebony and asked, "Ready to head back?"

"Yes. I'm ready," answered Audrey as she mounted Blaze. They trotted back to the corral in silence, each deep in thought about their possible upcoming search for their father.

They entered the corral; Brad dismounted, closed the gate, and then walked the horses in to the barn.

"I hope this packing and testing has been for naught," said Brad as he started unloading Ebony.

"Me too," added Audrey, removing the rifles and the rifle scabbards. "But like you said yesterday, it's better to test today and have time to fix the problems than to discover the problem when we're on the trail."

Ten minutes later, they had unloaded and unsaddled the horses. Brad carefully stacked the food and equipment in three stacks as before, one stack for each horse.

"The stack next to the door is for Blaze," said Brad. "The center stack is for Pa's horse, and the last one is for Ebony."

"Tomorrow we'll know if our efforts this morning have been worthwhile," said Audrey.

Brad looked at his sister, "Yes, tomorrow we'll know."

CHAPTER 5
THE POSSE RETURNS

Saturday, 23 October 1880: "It's Saturday afternoon," said Audrey. "Sheriff Tate said the posse would be back by now, at the latest. Let's go to his office. We can see Mr. Bates while we wait."

"Ma, I've filled the woodboxes and the kindling buckets," said Brad. "All my chores are done. Do you want us to get you anything while we're in town?"

"No, but do say hello to Jim for me. And, if the sheriff is late, don't say too long. I'll hold dinner for you."

"Thanks, Ma," said Audrey.

Brad saddled the horses while Audrey did the bridles. In a few minutes, they were riding toward Riverton. They stopped in front of Doc Adams' office, looped the reins over the rail, and ran up the steps.

"Glad to see you two again," said Mrs. Adams. "Jim is feeling better. Jake Jackson was here earlier and helped him stand up for the first time. Go in and say hello."

Brad and Audrey entered the room. Jim was sitting up in bed, reading the newspaper.

"Hello, Brad, Audrey," he said.

"Mrs. Adams told us you stood up today. You

look better, too. Her chicken soup must be working," said Audrey.

"Only when Jake was holding me," said Jim with a smile. "But I do feel much better. Tomorrow I'll be able to stand up without help, but only if Jake is here."

"You look better too," said Audrey.

"Any word from Denver?" asked Brad.

"Henry Morris stopped by earlier. He's the acting manager until your Pa comes back," said Jim.

Brad and Audrey talked with Mr. Bates until the sound of hoof-beats interrupted them.

"Sheriff Tate is back," announced Mrs. Adams looking out of the window. "They're getting off their horses now!"

"We're coming," replied Brad excitedly.

Brad and Audrey rushed down the stairs and looked at the posse. Sheriff Tate walked to them. His face was haggard and solemn.

"I'm sorry," said the sheriff. "We didn't find your father. We followed their tracks through rocks, streams, and the prairie. Then there was a small rain storm and we lost all traces."

"Thanks for trying," said Brad, a tear rolling down his cheek.

"Welcome back, Richard," said Reverend Wesley. "I came to hear about your search. I heard what you told Brad and Audrey. I'm sorry you couldn't find him."

"We searched Thursday afternoon, all day Friday, and again this morning," said Tom Shadden. "We just couldn't pick up their trail."

"Brad, Audrey, please come see me before you go home today," said Reverend Wesley.

"We can come now," said Audrey, tears running down her face.

Brad and Audrey un-looped the reins and joined the reverend, who waited for them a few yards north of the posse. The three of them walked down the street, Reverend Wesley in the center, the two horses following them. When they turned off Main Street, the reverend put a hand on each of their shoulders.

"It doesn't look good," he said. "I don't know the fate of your father. I've prayed for his safe return. But realize that the Lord doesn't always give us what we pray for. Come in and have some of my wife's cake and a cup of hot chocolate."

"We'd like to, but I'm not hungry," said Audrey.

"Maybe you'll change your mind when you see the cake," said the reverend. "I know the bad news about your father has ruined your appetite."

"Something may still turn up," said Brad, "but I doubt it."

They entered the parsonage and Mrs. Wesley saw their solemn faces. "They didn't find Harold, did they?"

"No, they didn't," replied the reverend. "We're going into the parlor to have a talk. Would you please bring us some of your cake and hot chocolate?"

"It'll be ready in a few minutes," she said.

Reverend Wesley motioned to a couple of chairs, "Please, have a seat."

Brad and Audrey sat down and looked at the reverend.

"Despite the pain you feel about your father, you must keep your faith. I may be wrong, but I believe that your father is still alive."

"We feel the same way," agreed Brad looking at his

sister. "Duke Badger is vicious. He is the kind of man who would hurt Pa and laugh about it. But, I don't believe that he would kill Pa outright. Duke likes to make people suffer. I believe Pa is still alive."

Reverend Wesley looked at Audrey and asked, "Do you believe that, too?"

"Yes, I do," said Audrey. "And so does Nana. When we talk to Ma about Pa, she cries and hugs us. She is really taking it hard."

"But Nana says that Ma also believes that Pa will come home," said Brad.

"I've prayed for your father," said the reverend. "And, in church tomorrow, I'll ask the folks to pray for him." The reverend paused, looked at Brad and Audrey, and then continued. "I'll also pray for the two of you."

"Here's the cake and hot chocolate," said Mrs. Wesley, holding a platter with three cups of hot chocolate and three large slices of chocolate cake.

"That does look good," observed Audrey.

Brad took a cup of hot chocolate and a small plate with the slice of cake. "I think my appetite's returned."

"Good, I don't like to eat alone," rejoined the reverend smiling. "Let me give a quick blessing."

After the blessing, they ate and talked about the challenges that lay ahead of them. Half an hour later they finished talking, and Brad and Audrey stood up to leave.

"Thanks for stopping by," said the reverend.

"Thanks for talking with us," replied Brad. "It feels better knowing that you understand why we're going to search for Pa."

50

Audrey stood up and said, "Please thank Mrs. Wesley for the cake and hot chocolate."

"It was great," said Brad as they started down the front steps.

"We got all our supplies yesterday," commented Audrey. "We'll leave at dawn tomorrow."

"May the Lord be with you," said the reverend as they mounted their horses.

When they got home, Brad and Audrey wiped down the horses and fed them some oats. Brad checked and oiled the bridles, saddles, and saddlebags. Audrey rechecked the supplies they had taken to the barn on Friday and those that they had added that morning.

She leaned against the barn door. "Everything is ready; do you still want to go tomorrow?"

"Yes," said Brad, "especially after our talks with Nana and Reverend Wesley. We're ready to get Pa."

As they walked to the house, Audrey related, "Nana will get us up early tomorrow morning. We can be on the road a little after sunup."

Brad stopped and faced his sister, "Audrey?"

"Yes?"

"I'm scared, but not like before. I know we'll find Pa."

"I'm scared, too," conceded his sister. "But I'm not too scared to search for Pa."

CHAPTER 6
THE SEARCH BEGINS

Sunday, 24 October 1880: Brad heard Nana go down the stairs to the kitchen. He slowly opened his eyes, looked out the window, and saw the light gray of pre-dawn pushing away the cloak of darkness. He quickly got up, washed his face, and combed his hair. This morning, he put on long underwear, then his jeans and a wool shirt. Winter was coming, and he knew he'd need long underwear in the mountains. He stopped at Audrey's door on the way to the kitchen and knocked. "Audrey, it's time to get up. I'll meet you in the kitchen. Nana went down a few minutes ago."

Audrey got up, rinsed her face, and brushed her hair. Like Brad, she dressed warmly. She put on woolen underwear, long wool stockings, a wool skirt, and a wool shirt. As she put on her boots, she said to herself, *I feel just like I did last night. I know we'll find Pa. I don't know how, but I know we'll find him.*

Audrey went downstairs and joined Brad and Nana in the kitchen. Nana had already built the fire in the cook stove, giving the kitchen a warm, cozy feeling.

"Both of you, come over here right now," said Nana.

Brad and Audrey gave each other a quizzical look

52

and went to Nana. "What is it?" asked Brad, stopping in front of his grandmother.

She put her arms around them and said, "I need to give you a squeeze and tell you that your mother and I love you. We're proud of you, too. After you went to bed last night, we talked about you and your father. While we want you to find your father, we also want you to stay home where it's safe. Now that I've said that, I'd better make breakfast and pack you a lunch," she said as a tear welled up in her eyes.

"We love you too, Nana," said Audrey, wrapping her arms around her grandmother.

"Thanks for helping us plan," said Brad, giving Nana a gentle bear hug.

"Are my Pinkertons bothering you, Victoria?" asked their mother as she entered the kitchen.

"No, we're just saying our good-byes while the stove is heating up."

"Well?" said their mother.

"Thanks for having faith in us," said Audrey as she went to her mother and put an arm around her.

"Me too," said Brad as he wrapped both of his arms around his mother.

"No need to get maudlin," said their grandmother. "Brad, I need some apples. Audrey, slice some bread for your sandwiches."

Nana was cooking the bacon and eggs in a pan. Pancakes sizzled on a large griddle as their mother sliced some roast venison for sandwiches. By the time breakfast was ready, the lunches were packed, and the table was set.

"Brad?"

Brad looked at Nana to see what she wanted, and then realized that she was asking him to say the blessing. Brad said a brief prayer and passed the platter of bacon and eggs to his mother.

"You have a long hard ride ahead of you," stated their mother. "Eat a good breakfast."

"Your grandmother and I reexamined your list of supplies last night, but we couldn't think of anything else to add. The sun is half-up," she said, looking out the kitchen window.

"This will be our last meal together for some time," said Nana. "Let us not rush."

The four of them talked about the supplies they had packed for their search as they ate. Their mother asked if they thought they needed more supplies, but they all agreed that they must travel light.

There was a lull in the conversation, and Nana nodded to the window. "The sun is just about up," she said. "You two had best get going. I'll do the dishes."

"Time to saddle the horses," said Brad opening the back door.

"I've got the lunches," said Audrey, picking up the two flour sacks with their sandwiches and apples.

They walked in silence to the barn. As soon as Brad opened the tack room door, Ebony came to him and nickered. Brad reached into his pocket and brought out the apples for the horses. Audrey put on the bridles while Brad began saddling the horses.

Brad broke the silence, "Ginger is learning. She's coming over for her saddle." Brad quickly saddled his father's horse and then started tying down the ax,

54

shovel, tarp, and other supplies. In a quarter of an hour the horses were ready to go.

"We're ready," said Brad, putting his father's rifle in his scabbard.

"I'm using your rifle," said Audrey. "It's lighter and has less kick than Pa's."

"I'll bring the horses; you get the gate," said Brad. He led the horses out of the corral and looped their reins over the hitching rail.

Audrey closed the gate and briefly looked at the house. "Nana and Ma are on the front porch."

"Let's mount up and wave good-bye," cautioned Brad as he mounted Ebony. "Nana said Ma will start crying if we say good-bye again."

Audrey handed Ginger's lead rope to her brother and then mounted Blaze.

"Let's start riding and wave good-bye before I cry too," warned his sister.

Brad looped his reins across the saddle horn and waved at Nana and his mother with his left hand as he clucked Ebony and tugged on the lead to his father's horse with his right. Audrey waved and squeezed Blaze's flanks with her heels. The horses broke into a gentle trot, three abreast. Brad was on the left, Audrey on the right, and their father's horse between them.

"We'll stay at a gentle trot to the stream. We can take a break there," said Brad.

The cold night air was beginning to warm, but there was still heavy dew on the grass. The hoofbeats of the three horses flushed out some pheasants which Brad and Audrey watched run across the road.

In an hour, they reached the site where the Big Foot

Gang had held up the stage five months earlier. A little later they reached the stream and stopped to water the horses.

"Let's ride up the stream a little to that clearing," suggested Brad. "I need to check the load on Pa's horse, and I don't want to do it on the road. I hear some rattling, and I may have to repack it."

Brad checked the saddlebags and found the cause. He worked in silence for a minute and then looked at Audrey. The can of kerosene was knocking against the hatchet. I wrapped the can with a flour sack. That should stop the noise."

"We certainly don't want to let Duke Badger hear us coming," agreed Audrey.

"Let's head on to the way station," he said, throwing a flat stone down the stream.

"It skipped three times," said Audrey. "Four times is your best, isn't it?"

"Yes, Running Bear has made five skips, so I have to keep practicing."

The break at the stream refreshed Brad and Audrey, as well as the horses. The sun was up and Brad unbuttoned his coat.

"It is getting a little warm," said Audrey as she unbuttoned her coat as well. "How about eating lunch on the hill that overlooks the holdup site?"

"Good idea," said Brad. "It'll be a good place to relax, and we can think like Duke Badger."

"And," said Audrey, "we can snack on Nana's oatmeal cookies."

It was late morning when they reached the curve just south of the way station. Audrey turned to her brother and suggested, "Brad, I'd just as soon not stop at the way station. I'd rather ride on to the holdup site and start searching. How about you?"

Brad thought for a moment. "You're right. We don't want anyone coming along to help us. We'll take the shortcut just before that stand of fir trees."

At the trees they turned left onto a narrow trail that passed west of the way station. A quarter of an hour later they were at the holdup site.

"Let's go to that clearing near the top of the hill. It's one of the highest spots in the area," said Brad.

Brad led the way. Ebony slowly climbed the rugged trail to the clearing. Brad tethered the horses while Audrey set out lunch.

"This will be the last of Nana's cooking until we get back," said Audrey.

"That's true," lamented Brad. "We should stop well before dusk, set up camp for the night, and build a small fire for supper. We want to have the fire out before dusk."

"If he looks for our campfire, he won't see it –because we won't have one," reasoned Audrey.

"True," agreed Brad. "Now, let's just eat, look, and think. Then we'll share our theories, even if we think we have a bad theory."

"Good idea," said his sister.

They ate Nana's roast venison sandwiches in silence while studying the hills and plains. There were mountains behind them, as well as to the north. Looking straight ahead to the east, there were uninhabited plains. Riverton was to the south. After several minutes, Audrey broke the silence.

"I think they went east. To the north there is Denver, Sheriff Strong, and possible army patrols. If he goes west, he enters the mountains, and winter is coming. Riverton and Sheriff Tate are to the south. That leaves the east with open plains and gentle foothills. What do think he'd do, Brad?"

"If I were Duke Badger, I'd go east too. There, I can hole up in a valley or small canyon in the foothills. My gang can build a simple ranch house, barn, and corral. And, we can easily ride out to rob banks, stages, and rustle a few head of cattle from the ranchers."

Audrey looked north and continued. "They took the road north when they took . . .," Audrey paused and choked back a sob, "when they took Pa."

"If we ride east four or five miles, and then turn north, we should cross their trail. What do you think?"

"I think that's what Running Bear would do," agreed Audrey.

"We'd better check our rifles again," suggested Brad. "We don't want to get in a gun-fight with the Badger Gang. But, if we do run in to them and they start shooting, we'd best be ready."

"I know you're right, Brad, but I don't think I could shoot a person, even Duke Badger."

Brad looked at his sister's tearful face for a moment, and then said, "I don't want you to either. We want to follow their trail, but not let them know it."

Brad and Audrey mounted up and slowly went down the narrow trail to the road. Brad dismounted and quickly checked the loads on the horses. Then they traveled north about half a mile when Brad stopped.

"This looks like a good place to head east," he said.

"We'll find a good landmark, and then turn north to cross their trail," added Audrey.

Brad reined Ebony east off of the road and continued, "Let's get started."

Audrey followed, and they rode side by side about five miles to a slight rise. Brad stopped, looked north for a minute, and said, "We'll aim for that notch in the mountain. I'll look to the left; you look to the right."

They rode in silence as they studied the ground for recent signs of horses. After about an hour, they both stopped, and looked at each other knowingly. Audrey was the first to speak. "Bear was right. Even though it rained, it looks like eight to ten horses passed through here several days ago."

Brad got off his horse and carefully examined the tracks. "And, the horses were shod." Brad led Ebony as he followed the trail on foot for a few minutes. "One set of hoofprints is deeper than the others. The horse was probably carrying two men - the outlaw and Pa."

"Mount up. Let's go," said Audrey.

Brad mounted and the horses broke into a slow trot. In an hour, they approached another slight rise. Brad reined Ebony back to a walk, and Audrey did the same with Blaze. Brad stopped, dismounted, and handed his reins to Audrey; then he crawled up behind a lone tree near the top of the rise. After carefully examining what lay ahead, Brad stood up and motioned Audrey to join him. Audrey clucked Blaze forward, holding Ebony's reins in her left hand. Ginger followed as her lead rope was tied to Ebony.

"Audrey, take a look. There's a grove of trees about

a mile ahead. It would be a good place to camp for the night, don't you think?"

Audrey halted the horses beside her brother and handed him Ebony's reins. She studied the landscape for a minute and replied, "It looks good. It's well away from the Badger Gang's trail, it's at the side of a hill, and there's probably a small stream or a spring in the trees."

"With the trees, we can make a shelter for the night," said Brad.

"I brought the potatoes. Can you get a pheasant?" asked Audrey, smiling for the first time that day.

"We'll find out," answered Brad as he mounted Ebony.

Ten minutes later, they reached the small grove of trees. Brad checked the area and found a nice site next to a small stream. Their campsite was in a dense cluster of trees with a small clearing in the middle. They tethered the horses and starting setting up camp. Brad cut down a large sapling and lodged it between two small trees. He tied one side of the tarp to the sapling. Audrey watched as he tied the other end of the tarp to the base of two other trees.

"That should keep us dry if it rains tonight," said Brad.

While he was preparing the shelter, Audrey dug their fire pit. "I've placed the rocks and have some wood for the fire. And," she said enthusiastically, "I saw some fish jumping in the stream. We brought some fishhooks; how about fish for supper?"

"Good. We wouldn't announce our presence with a gun shot," concluded Brad. "I'll dig some worms while you get the hooks."

A few minutes later, Brad had a couple of worms, and Audrey had the fishhooks and line connected to two stout sticks, each stick about five feet long.

"I'll bait your hook first," said Brad, putting a wriggling worm on his sister's hook.

Audrey threw the hook into the water and waited. While Brad was baiting his hook, Audrey's line started moving. "I've got one!" she exclaimed.

"Pull it in while I put my line in," said Brad.

Audrey pulled on the stick and the fish broke water. "It looks pretty big."

"They all look big in the water," said Brad, tossing his hook into the water. "Wait till you get it out."

Audrey pulled the fish out onto the bank and Brad looked at it, and then at his sister. "It is a big one."

Audrey pointed at Brad's line moving up the stream. "You've got one, too!" Brad yanked the stick and a fish a little bit smaller than his sister's flopped onto the bank.

"We have dinner," he proclaimed with satisfaction. "I'll start the fire."

Brad gathered a few fistfuls of dry grass and twigs, put them in the fire pit, and struck a match. The grass and twigs quickly caught fire. He added more twigs and some small sticks and branches his sister had gathered. In a few minutes, the fire was burning nicely, and he placed two thick tree branches on it.

"I'll clean the fish while you collect some more wood for the fire," said Brad. "We'll have a nice fish dinner."

"We have everything but lemonade," said Audrey.

Audrey had ringed the fire pit with rocks earlier and arranged some rocks inside it so she could set the skillet on them. With a butcher knife, she cut two slices off of the slab of bacon and put them in the large cast iron skillet. Then she put the skillet on the rocks, cut the potatoes into slices, and added them to the bacon.

"The bacon smells good," said Brad returning from the stream. "Here's the fish. I'll cut some fir branches for us to sleep on."

Brad gathered several armloads of small fir branches to place under their blankets. He had their saddles and blankets in the tarp lean-to by the time Audrey took the skillet off the fire.

"The fish and potatoes are ready," she said. "How are our beds?"

"They're not as nice as home, but we shouldn't be too uncomfortable tonight."

Audrey put the fish and potatoes on their tin plates and looked at Brad.

"I'm famished," he confessed as he forked a large piece of fish to his mouth. His chewing slowed, and he looked at his sister, "This is good. No, it's not good, it's great."

"It sure is," she agreed. "The fact that we're hungry, tired, and away from home probably helps."

Brad forked another piece, "That may be true, but I don't care. I'm eating and enjoying it."

When they finished, they leaned back against their saddles and peered at the late afternoon sun in the western sky. A gentle gust of wind swirled a few leaves in front of the campfire.

Audrey looked at her brother, "It's starting to get chilly; I'm glad we brought extra blankets."

"It's going to get even colder," stated Brad. "I hope we find Pa soon."

"Do you still believe we'll find Pa. . . alive?" asked Audrey in a hoarse voice.

Brad stood up with their plates, looked at his sister a moment, and firmly replied, "Yes, I do. We'll find Pa and take him home."

Brad took the plates to the stream and washed them while Audrey cleaned the skillet. They returned to their camp, and Brad got the coffeepot. He went back to the stream, rinsed it, and filled it with water.

"Brad," Audrey protested in disbelief. "We don't drink coffee; why are you filling the coffeepot?"

"I brought some tea. Would you like a cup?"

"No. You're making it in the coffeepot, and it will taste awful."

Brad grinned at his sister and replied, "No it won't. Nana and I cleaned it last week. Now would you like a cup of tea?"

"In that case, yes, and with two lumps, please," she giggled.

"Yes m'lady. Two lumps. Tea will be served in the library just in front of your saddle."

When the water boiled, Brad added a large pinch of tea and pulled the pot out of the fire. While the tea steeped, Brad kicked some dirt on the glowing embers in the fire pit, waited a bit, and then filled two tin mugs with tea, handing one to his sister.

"This isn't a library, but the tea is good," said Audrey, glancing at the setting sun. "This has been a long day. Right now, I'm so tired I can hardly keep my eyes open."

"Tomorrow will be even longer," he said. "Go ahead

and get some sleep. I put some tree limbs and rocks on each side of the lean-to. That'll protect us from the wind. I've also hobbled the horses. I don't expect to be bothered by wolves or Duke Badger, but just in case, I put our rifles under our blankets."

"Let's talk about breakfast," suggested Audrey. "We can have cookies and apples for breakfast, or I can make bacon, fried potatoes, and pancakes. What would you like?"

"That's no choice," claimed Brad. "I'll take the bacon, potatoes, and pancakes. We'd better save the oatmeal cookies and apples for lunch, possibly even supper. Go ahead and go to sleep. I'll make sure the fire is out before dark. But first, I'll get ready for the morning fire. There's some dry grass and twigs under my saddle."

"I'll hold your tea," said Audrey, reaching for her brother's mug as he stood up.

Brad walked into the trees next to their shelter and started picking up small branches. Returning, he stacked them under his saddle with the grass and twigs he had gathered earlier.

Brad settled down and leaned back against his saddle. "Now, I'm ready for the fire."

"Remember when we camped with Pa last month?" recalled his sister. "This is just as good, and the fish were just as tasty as the pheasant."

Brad took a sip of tea. "True, but with the cold weather, the hot tea is better than the lemonade."

"Now I know how Pa could go to sleep so fast," said Audrey. "If you're tired enough, a blanket on some fir boughs with a saddle behind your head makes a very nice bed."

"I'll see you in the morning," Brad said, drinking the last of the tea in his mug.

Audrey pulled the blanket around her and closed her eyes. Brad looked at his sister and the ashes in the fire pit. Through the trees, he watched the sun slowly slip behind the distant mountains. Like a lamp burning the last of its kerosene, the darkness of the night replaced the fading twilight.

CHAPTER 7
HIDING FROM DUKE BADGER

Monday Morning, 25 October 1880: Brad pulled the blanket up around his neck and reached for his pillow. He didn't find the pillow, but his hand hit something hard, and it wasn't the wall. The gurgle of the stream connected with his consciousness and he remembered that he and Audrey had spent the night in their makeshift camp, searching for their father. He opened his eyes to pre-dawn grayness and knew that the sun would be rising in a few minutes. He turned his boots upside down and shook them, checking to be sure nothing came out. He put them on and looked at his sister, wrapped in her blanket, still asleep.

Brad quietly got up, pulled the dry grass, twigs, and small branches from under his saddle, quickly laid the fire, and then struck a match. Cupping his hands around the small flame, he touched it to the dry grass and small twigs. He watched the fire consume the grass and ignite the twigs before adding more twigs and some pinecones. A minute later, he added a few small branches.

Audrey mumbled something in her sleep as Brad picked up the coffeepot. He quietly left the shelter, went to the stream, and filled the coffeepot with water. As he set it on the rocks in the fire pit, Audrey groaned, turned over, and sat up.

"Good morning m'lady," said Brad. "Your tea will be served shortly."

"Brad, you'll make some woman a fine husband. You get up early, start the fire, and boil the tea water while she sleeps. When you've decided whom you wish to marry, let me know. I'll tell her all about your skills. If she's smart, she'll say yes before you even finish proposing."

"I'll remember that when I find Miss Future Wife. This morning, however, I happened to wake up early, so I started the fire. We can probably be on the trail in an hour. I'll get the skillet and start the bacon and potatoes while you make the pancakes."

When the water began boiling, Brad added a big pinch of tea and set the pot away from the fire. He looked at his sister mixing the pancake batter. She held the tin bowl between her knees as she stirred and added water to get the right consistency.

"Bacon and potatoes are on the plates. The skillet is ready for the pancakes," said Brad.

"They'll be army pancakes," replied Audrey. "No eggs, no buttermilk, and no butter, but I do have some maple syrup."

Brad nodded his head knowingly. "So, we'll finally find out what Pa means when he talks about army pancakes."

Audrey poured four circles of batter in the large skillet and put the skillet back over the fire. When the bubbles broke on the pancakes, she turned them with the butcher knife. A minute later, the pancakes were ready.

As usual, they ate in silence for a minute before talking.

"The bacon and potatoes are good," Audrey said.

"These pancakes aren't so bad, either. Why did Pa complain about them?"

"His didn't have baking soda and cream of tartar to make them rise like ours. Army pancakes only had flour."

As soon as he finished eating, Brad took the dishes and skillet to the creek to wash them. By the time he returned, Audrey had rolled up their blankets.

"I'll get the horses ready while you pack. We can finish our tea before we mount up," said Brad.

Brad saddled the horses and firmly tied their supplies behind the saddles.

"The load on Ginger looks smaller," noted Audrey. "Lunch, supper, breakfast, and oats for the horses last night made a difference."

"We still have oatmeal cookies and apples in our saddlebags for lunch, and possibly supper," said Brad.

Audrey put the tin mugs in her saddlebags and continued, "We can always eat the canned beans cold; we don't have to heat them."

"Let's water the horses and then go back to the trail," said Brad.

They walked to the stream, and Audrey thought about the day ahead while the horses drank their fill. When Blaze had finished drinking, she tossed her head and snorted.

"She's ready to go," said Audrey.

"So are Ebony and Ginger," said her brother.

Audrey touched Brad's arm. "Thanks for your prayer this morning. I feel much better."

"So do I," he said, gently nudging Ebony in the flanks.

Ebony snorted, bobbed her head, and immediately broke into a comfortable trot. Soon the horses were aligned side by side. They headed south from the campsite to the tracks of the Badger Gang.

"Here we are," observed Brad, reining Ebony to a stop. "I'll watch the tracks. You keep a lookout to the east. We don't want to ride into Duke Badger's camp."

"If I see anything unusual, I'll stop and we can talk about it," confirmed his sister. "Two sets of eyes are better than one."

A little bit later, Brad commented, "I'm concerned about the weather. The horses are excited. They both snorted excitedly this morning, and Ebony's been bobbing her head a lot more than usual. Look to the west. There are white clouds rushing toward us, and it's colder than yesterday. I think there's a storm coming. If I'm right, it may start snowing this afternoon."

Audrey looked to the west and agreed. "We'd better travel fast. Once it starts snowing, their tracks will be covered."

"Come on Ebony, let's go," said Brad as he gently pressed his horse's flanks. Ebony immediately broke into a comfortable lope. The other horses followed, and again they aligned themselves three abreast.

Every time they came to the crest of a hill, they'd stop. Brad would crawl to the top and look for signs of the Badger Gang before they continued.

Around noon, they came to another gentle rise, one

of many that morning. Audrey said, "We'd better stop and scout it out. Duke's camp could always be on the other side."

They reined to a stop; Brad dismounted and crept to the top of the rise. "Audrey, bring the horses. Come take a look."

Audrey rode up behind Brad, dismounted, and handed him Ebony's reins. In the distance was a thin column of smoke.

"A campfire?" queried Audrey.

Brad nodded his head. "It's three to four miles from here, but the tracks we're following lead right to it."

Brad pointed to his left. "About a mile or so ahead are some trees by that hill. Let's go there. I'll climb to the top and get a good look at the source of that smoke."

Brad and Audrey remounted and veered left to the base of the hill.

As they approached the hill, Brad pointed to an area sheltered by some large boulders and a stand of trees. Audrey entered the clearing first and reined Blaze to a halt.

"That hill is pretty steep; it's more like a butte," said Brad. "Stay here, and I'll try to find a way to the top."

They dismounted and tethered the horses. Brad examined the butte and finally selected the route he would take to the top. Audrey waited while Brad started climbing. It was too steep for a horse, but it seemed like a path. Brad took a while to reach the top.

He stood at the top of the butte. "The Indians probably used this spot as a lookout," he said to himself. He looked closer; where he stood, the earth was black. "They built fires here to send smoke signals."

Audrey looked up the steep hill and thought, *Brad is right, maybe it should be called a butte.* She saw Brad at the top waving to her, so she waved back.

"Well," Brad said to himself, "let's see what's making that smoke." In the distance, he could see men on horses. He looked carefully and counted seven men. *Well, at least I think they're men, but they're so small, they could be mice.* The smoke from the campfire disappeared. He continued watching as two horsemen rode away from the grove of trees. *They're coming this way; I've got to tell Audrey. We've got to hide.*

Brad picked up a small rock and threw it in the trees behind Audrey. Audrey looked up, and Brad slapped his hat against his thigh. Then he acted as if he were shooting a pistol.

Brad must be telling me to get ready for trouble, Audrey realized.

"Blaze," she said, "let's find a place to hide while Brad's coming down."

Audrey mounted Blaze and left Ebony and Ginger. She rode up the edge of the hill that Brad was on. There were trees and some narrow paths. Audrey took one of the paths. A minute later, she followed the path between some boulders and suddenly found herself at the entrance to a large cave. Turning around, she rode back through the boulders and took the wider, lower trail. That trail passed in front of the cave, but bushes and large boulders hid its entrance.

"Blaze, I think we've found our hiding place," she said. "Let's go tell Brad. If he was telling me the Badger Gang is coming, we've got to hide, and hide now."

Brad was just about down when Audrey rode up.

"Audrey! We've got to hide. Some men are riding this way. They're probably members of the Badger Gang."

"I've found a cave to hide in!" she told him. "Bring the horses and follow me."

Brad quickly mounted Ebony. Ginger's lead rope was still tied to his saddle horn, and he clucked Ebony to a trot.

"Take the narrow high path," ordered Audrey pointing to her right. "As soon as we go between those large boulders, there's a large cave. It's big enough to hold the horses."

Audrey reined Blaze between the two boulders. Brad hesitated and followed. It was a very narrow path. He had just gone through the boulders when Ebony suddenly stopped. The lead rope to Ginger was taut.

"Audrey, take Ebony. I've got to check Pa's horse."

Brad dismounted, untied the lead rope, and went back to the boulders. Ginger was stuck; she was older and wider. In addition, the shovel and ax she carried made her too wide to go between the boulders. Brad quickly untied the them, ran back between the boulders, and tossed them into the cave.

Returning to Ginger he pleaded, "Come on, girl, you've got to fit now. Duke Badger may be here any minute." The horse balked, but Brad tugged, and Ginger slowly squeezed between the boulders.

"Wrap their muzzles," said Brad, bringing his father's horse into the giant cave. "We can't let the horses nicker and give us away. I'm going to block the path between those boulders."

Brad ran back to the boulders, looked around, and saw some dead tree branches. He studied them a moment before grabbing a large branch and pulling it between the boulders. Then he pulled a slightly smaller branch on top of the large one. Hearing horses and men talking, he rushed back to the cave.

"Duke, let's take the lower path; the one between those boulders is narrow, and it's blocked," said a man.

"Lutz, we have to see who came here. They might have been following us," said Duke.

"We haven't seen anyone Duke. Besides, who's going to follow us? It's been five days since we held up the stage. The posse left a couple of days ago without finding our trail."

"I know someone was following us, Lutz; I can feel it. We also saw some tracks coming this way. If we see someone, plug em'. We don't take any chances."

Audrey stood about ten feet inside the cave holding the horses' bridles. Her rifle was by her left foot, propped against the wall of the cave.

Brad knelt on one knee about five feet inside the entrance of the cave behind a big rock. He'd already taken off his hat and levered a round into the chamber of his rifle, pointing it toward the cave entrance. He could hear Duke and Lutz talking.

"Duke, there's a storm coming. The wind's picking up, and we've still got a few hours ride to our hideout. Let's go."

"Lutz, climb up those rocks and see what's behind those bushes. Someone could hide there. I'll cover ya'."

Brad heard Lutz climbing up the rocks and saw hands grab a large bush. Lutz's dirty gray hat and black hair slowly rose from behind the bush.

"It's a cave, Duke. Want to go in?"

"No, there could be a bear in there this time of year. Get down. Maybe you're right; let's go."

Brad heard the sound of falling rocks as Lutz went down the hill to his horse.

"Let's get the rest of the men, leave that Benton guy for the wolves, and get out of here," growled Duke.

Brad heard the men ride away. He waited a minute and cautiously edged to the entrance of the cave with his rifle. Listening carefully, he crawled out and looked through the bushes. No one was there. Looking up and down the trail, he saw nothing. Brad slowly stood up and looked again before returning to the cave.

"Audrey," said Brad entering the cave. "It was Duke Badger and Lutz Hall. Did you hear them say they saw our tracks and that they have Pa? Duke said they were going to leave Pa for the wolves."

"We're not going to leave Pa to the wolves," snapped his sister.

"Let's ride back to that clearing again. I'll climb to the top of the hill and see what they're doing. Now that I know the way, I can make the climb a lot faster."

Audrey brought the horses out of the cave while Brad removed the branches that blocked the narrow path. In a few minutes, they were riding back toward the clearing. The sky was darkening, and a few flakes of snow were falling by the time they reached the base of the butte.

"Watch the horses," said Brad, jumping off Ebony. "I'll hurry so I can get down before the snow starts sticking."

Brad practically ran up the side of the butte. He was breathless when he reached the top. Gasping for air, he took off his hat and went to the other side of the hilltop. He saw men breaking camp and saddling their horses. Brad watched for a minute and noticed that more snowflakes were falling, and some were sticking.

Audrey watched Brad come to the edge of the hilltop, wave his hat, and then start down. Halfway down, she saw Brad slip and fall.

"Brad!" she screamed.

Brad got up, brushed off his pants, and continued coming down the hill, but more slowly. As he neared the bottom, Audrey rushed toward him.

"Brad, are you hurt?"

"No, just bruised and scratched. I slipped on a little patch of snow."

"What did you see?" she asked.

"The gang is breaking camp and saddling their horses. They're getting ready to leave. If we ride through the trees along the side of the hill, they probably won't see us."

"Let's do it," agreed Audrey. "It may be slower, but it's safer."

The wind was picking up, and a few heavy snowflakes whipped around them as they mounted their horses. They rode next to the base of the hill and were just short of the trees when Audrey put up her hand and stopped.

"Brad!" she exclaimed. "Did you hear a shot?"

"Yes! Forget the trees. Let's go directly to their campsite. Have your rifle ready."

Brad kicked Ebony's flanks and leaned forward in the saddle. Ebony sensed the urgency and immediately broke into a gallop. Audrey followed with Ginger. As Brad came up a small draw, he reined Ebony to a halt, pulled his rifle from its scabbard, and jumped to the ground in one fluid motion. He ran in a crouch through the prairie grass toward the crest of the hill at the top of the draw. By the time he reached the top, Audrey was behind him with her rifle. The rise overlooked the gang's campsite a quarter-of-a-mile away. The Badger Gang was gone.

CHAPTER 8
PA IS FOUND

In the distance, a man stood with his back to tree, a pack of wolves slowly moving toward him. Through the blowing snow, Brad could see the man holding a large stick in his right hand, his left arm hanging at his side.

"That's Pa," shouted Brad over the soft howl of the wind. "The wolves are going to attack him."

Brad rested his rifle on a rock and sighted on the wolf closest to his father. "Lord, please help me shoot straight. Don't let me shoot Pa."

"Remember what he taught us," reminded Audrey as she levered a shell into her rifle.

"Take your time, gently squeeze the trigger," advised Brad. "I'll take those on the left. You take the right, and remember to adjust for the wind."

The rifles kicked into their shoulders, the sound of their shots muffled by the howling wind and the falling snow.

"I got one," said Brad.

"Me too," said Audrey.

"Pa's a good teacher," said Brad, levering another shell into his rifle.

Brad and Audrey put two more wolves in their sights

and squeezed the triggers again. Two more wolves fell; the rest of the pack turned and ran.

"Let's go," said Brad. "Pa needs us."

Brad and Audrey put their rifles in their rifle boots, mounted their horses, and galloped toward their father. It was getting colder, and the snowflakes stuck to their clothes as they raced across the snow-streaked grassy plain. The horses sensed the urgency and galloped as fast as they could. The ride seemed like an eternity to Brad and Audrey as they saw their father slowly slump to the ground. Brad reached their father first and reined Ebony to a halt.

"Pa!" yelled Brad, jumping off his horse. "It's Brad and Audrey!"

Audrey was right behind her brother. She jumped off and rushed to her father, tears streaming down her face. "Pa, please don't die!" she cried.

"I knew you'd come," said their father, shivering from the cold.

"Brad looked at the spreading red patch on his father's torn and dirty shirt. Touching the wound, he felt the sticky warmth of blood and his father's shudder of pain. "Duke shot you!"

"Your shoes are gone, too," cried Audrey, staring at his feet.

"He said there was no need to waste good shoes on wolf food, so he took my shoes. As they rode away, he stopped, pulled his pistol, and shot me, just like he shot Jim Bates."

"Audrey, I'll get the bandages and carbolic acid. You get Pa's fresh clothes and some blankets. Then we've got to make a shelter. The way that wind is blowing with those dark clouds, we're going to have a real blizzard."

"It's just like Jim's wound," Brad observed as he uncorked the bottle of carbolic acid.

"Here's some blankets, Pa," said Audrey, wrapping them around her father.

"Those blankets sure feel nice," whispered their father as he winced from the carbolic acid.

Brad quickly pressed a clean kerchief to the wound and said, "We need to get you into your long johns, Pa. You'll freeze without them."

"I've got them right here," said Audrey. "Then we've got to build a shelter and a fire."

Brad and Audrey helped him into his long underwear, wool pants, wool shirt, socks, and boots. Audrey held out his coat. "Here's your sheepskin coat and hat."

Brad looked around and selected a place to build the shelter where some bushes and trees grew next to a large boulder. Brad took the ax, cut a small sapling, and removed its branches. Then he placed one end in the crook of a large tree and the other end between another tree and the boulder.

"Audrey, get some grass and shake the snow off it. Put the grass, some twigs and pine needles under a blanket. We'll need them to start the fire."

Audrey gathered grass and twigs while Brad worked on the lean-to. The snow was thick and falling in large heavy flakes by the time he finished the shelter.

"Here's the tarp," said Audrey. "I've got the grass and twigs under Pa's blanket."

Brad and Audrey tied the tarp to the large sapling that Brad had placed between the tree and the boulders.

"Let's put Pa in the lean-to," said Brad, tying the last portion of the tarp to the sapling. "Then we'll start the fire."

Audrey and Brad helped their father stand up and walk to the lean-to. Audrey helped him get comfortable and covered him with some blankets while Brad worked to finish their shelter.

"I knew you and Brad would come looking for me, but when Duke shot me and rode off, I thought it was the end. I prayed that you'd find me before the wolves did."

"Pa, I'm going to get some fir boughs to put under our blankets. Brad's getting more branches to put on top of the shelter."

"Do you have anything to eat?" asked her father. "I'm starved."

"Here's an apple while we do our work," said Audrey pulling one out of her coat pocket.

Brad cut more tree limbs for the roof of the lean-to while Audrey took the hatchet and cut small fir boughs to put under their blankets. Fortunately, the large boulder and bushes helped Brad make the shelter quickly. When he was finished, the lean-to was about ten feet wide, eight feet deep, and six feet high.

"I'll unsaddle the horses and tether them," said Brad. "Can you get the rifles and supplies?"

"We'll be right back, Pa," said Audrey.

She unloaded the rifles and supplies and put them in the lean-to while Brad removed the saddles. Together they helped their father sit up so Brad could put the saddle behind his father's head. Then Audrey helped him lay back and tucked the blankets around him. Her brother tethered the horses in the sheltered area beside the lean-to.

When her father was settled, Audrey took the shovel and dug a shallow hole near the front of the shelter. She placed some rocks she had collected earlier in the fire pit to hold the skillet and the coffeepot. Reaching under the saddle, she pulled out the grass and twigs for the fire.

"The grass is wet," groaned Audrey. "We can't use it for the fire."

"That's why I brought the kerosene," laughed Brad. "Lay the twigs and small branches while I get some firewood."

Brad remembered he had seen a fallen tree beside a large pine tree. It was now covered with an inch of snow. Brad brushed the snow off a portion of the fallen tree and began chopping. A few minutes later, he returned with an armload of wood.

"The fire's laid," said Audrey as Brad straightened the tarp.

I'll add a little kerosene and then light it," said her brother.

Audrey nodded at their father lying against his saddle, fast asleep. "He went right to sleep. He said he hasn't had anything to eat for two days, so I gave him an apple. He ate it, core and all."

"When we get the fire going, we can make some tea, maybe even some army pancakes," said Brad.

He poured a little bit of kerosene on the twigs and small branches. Audrey watched as he carefully put the cap back on the can, tightened it, and returned it to the saddlebag. He struck a match on the edge of his father's dry boot to light the fire. The kerosene quickly caught, even though a few flakes of snow dropped through the small opening at the top of the lean-to, sizzling when they hit the flames.

"The snow is really starting to coming down," said Brad. "Hopefully the storm will be over tomorrow. Then we can start home."

"When Pa taught us how to make a shelter, I never thought we would actually have to make one," he said while watching the fire burn.

"Neither did I, especially during a blizzard with wolves close by and Pa wounded."

"And at the Badger Gang's last campsite," added her brother.

"Particularly with the Badger Gang still in the area," emphasized Brad.

"How much wood do we have?" asked Audrey, adding two small pieces to the fire.

"About four hours, perhaps a little more," he responded. "Keep the fire small, just enough to cook with and to keep the chill out. I'll get some more wood."

Audrey watched Brad push the tarp aside as he left the lean-to. Her father was snoring softly. She got out the skillet, coffeepot, bacon, and flour. Then she adjusted the rocks with the hatchet so she could cook over the small fire. Their father was still sleeping when Brad returned with his third armload of wood.

"That should take care of us until tomorrow afternoon," he said, brushing the snow off his jacket.

"We'll need water too," added Audrey. "Did you see a stream, or should we melt snow?"

"There should be a stream, but I didn't see or hear it."

"You watch Pa," she said. "Warm yourself; I'll find the stream and get some water."

Audrey took the coffeepot and their empty canteens, snugged-up her coat, and pushed back the tarp. A blast of wind rushed at her, and big wet snowflakes splattered against her warm face.

"The snow really is coming down," she said. "I'll be right back."

"Get your bearings and walk down hill," advised her brother. "Walk a straight line. If you get lost, stop and holler. I'll listen for you."

"I will; you take care of Pa."

Audrey pushed the tarp back into place, stood still for a minute, and listened for a stream. All she heard was the wind. Looking to her left, she saw a curving string of bushes at the bottom of a slope. *The stream is probably the other side of those bushes*, she thought. Audrey looked for a landmark next to the lean-to and selected the big pine tree.

In a few minutes, she found the stream. She quickly filled the coffeepot and canteens, stood up to get her bearings and started back up the slope.

"Pa, you're awake," said Brad. "Audrey went to find a stream to get water. She'll be back in a minute."

"Take a rifle, and go get her," ordered his father. "She may run into the wolves. They were close last night. They made everyone edgy, except Duke."

"I forgot all about the wolves," Brad exclaimed, grabbing a rifle. He buttoned-up his jacket, pushed the tarp aside with his rifle, and left the lean-to. The wind was increasing, and the blowing snow made it hard to see.

"Audrey!" he shouted. He waited for a reply but heard nothing. *She probably went to the left*, he thought. There was a string of bushes at the bottom of the slope. Brad went to his left, walked several feet, stopped, and again shouted his sister's name.

Audrey climbed to the top of the slope and stopped. The snow whirled around her as she tried to see the large pine tree. *I've got to find my way back*, she thought. *We found Pa. I can't get lost and freeze to death, not now.*

Brad squinted as the wind-driven snow pelted his face and eyes. Again he shouted Audrey's name. Staring into the falling snow, Brad realized that his sister would never be able to hear him over the howling wind.

Audrey stood still and asked herself what Running Bear would do. *He'd say walk in a straight line from the shelter to the stream, and then return in a straight line.* Audrey could faintly see the string of bushes near the stream. *I'm returning the way I came*, she said to herself. *I'll continue in a straight line another ten steps, and then call for Brad.*

Brad saw some movement in the swirling snow. He thought to himself, *that is either wolves, or Audrey. I'll call her again.*

Audrey stopped, looking again for the large pine tree, but saw nothing. "Brad!" she shouted. Then she listened carefully for a reply, but heard nothing.

"Audrey!" shouted Brad. He listened, but heard nothing. Then he levered a round into his rifle, pointed it into the air, and fired.

"Brad!" shouted Audrey after she heard the shot. "Brad!"

He heard what he thought was Audrey's voice and again shouted, "Audrey!" He saw movement to his left again, and took a few steps toward the dark form moving in the swirling snow.

Audrey heard a snarling growl and saw two wolves in front of her. "Brad!" she screamed, "Wolves!"

Brad saw the outline of a wolf and heard it snarl. He quickly levered in a fresh cartridge, aimed, and fired. The wolf instantly dropped to the ground and didn't move. The other wolf ran away.

"Brad!" Audrey shouted. "Here I am!"

Brad saw the silhouette of a person carrying something moving toward him. "Audrey!" he shouted.

Audrey saw a man with a rifle and knew it had to be her brother. "Brad!" she shouted in reply as she saw her brother. "I got lost. The falling snow is so thick; I couldn't see to find my way back."

Brad grasped her arm, turned around, and started back to the lean-to. "Pa told me to bring a rifle because of the wolves. I'm glad I did."

Twenty steps later they reached the lean-to. Audrey pulled back the tarp and they both went in. Their father looked up at them expectantly.

"A couple of wolves almost got me!" exclaimed Audrey.

"I heard their snarl just after I saw Audrey," said Brad. "I shot one and the other left."

"Thank goodness you got back safely," their father said. "I'm too weak to go searching for you."

Audrey looked at her father wrapped in blankets, resting against his saddle. "After all that trouble for the water, let's have dinner. I'll make some tea, cook some bacon, and make some . . ." Audrey paused and looked at her father and smiled before continuing, "I'll make some army pancakes."

Her father grinned and replied, "Right now, army pancakes sound real nice."

Brad added a piece of wood to the fire. Audrey sliced a few pieces of bacon into the skillet and placed it on the small fire. Next, she poured some of the flour mixture Nana had made into the tin bowl, added some water from a canteen, and stirred.

Brad put the coffeepot on the rocks at the edge of the fire and warmed his hands. "Running Bear said to keep the fire small, then you can keep warm," said Brad.

"He's right," replied his father.

"I didn't think the wolves would be out in a blizzard," said Brad.

"True. Wolves usually hole up during a blizzard. Those wolves were probably trying to get back with their pack. I doubt that they'll be out tonight."

Audrey moved the bacon to the edge of the skillet and then spooned in some batter. "The pancakes will be ready in a few minutes," she said.

Brad added some tea to the water that had started boiling in the coffeepot and set the pot on the ground at the edge of the fire.

"The tea will be ready when the pancakes are," he said. "I'll get the mugs and plates."

Brad searched the saddlebags and found what they needed. Audrey put the pancakes and bacon on the plates, handed one to her father, and held the other two while Brad added a can of beans to the skillet.

"Army pancakes," announced Audrey, setting a plate in front of her brother.

Brad filled the mugs with tea and said, "Benton tea, Pa," as he handed a mug to his father and one to Audrey. "It's better than the Riverton Hotel's special blend of coffee."

"There's no syrup for the pancakes. I thought we had two cans, but I can't find them," said Audrey.

"Army pancakes don't have syrup," stated her father between mouthfuls. "And they never tasted this good either."

When they had finished the pancakes, Audrey spooned the hot beans onto their plates.

"I haven't eaten much, but I'm full," said their father, leaning back against his saddle.

"That's because you haven't eaten for days," said Brad. He reached into his pocket. "Take this oatmeal cookie in case you wake up in the middle of the night."

"Here's another one," said Audrey, handing him a cookie wrapped in wax paper.

Brad added another piece of wood to the fire and refilled everyone's mug with tea. The wind whipped against their shelter, and flakes of snow fell through the smoke hole, sizzling as they hit the fire. Brad and Audrey looked at their father wrapped in blankets with a mug of tea in his hand, leaning back against his saddle.

"Keep the rifles ready, just in case," ordered their father, setting down his empty mug and closing his eyes. "With the blizzard outside, Duke probably won't come back tonight. But, then again, he does some mighty strange things."

CHAPTER 9
THE MORNING AFTER THE STORM

Tuesday, 26 October 1880: Audrey heard the tarp flapping in the wind and opened her eyes. She pulled the blanket tightly around her body and looked around the shelter. The fire was still smoldering, so Brad or their father must have added wood several times during the night. She crawled over to the small stack of wood, got a couple of pieces, and put them on the fire. The wind was still blowing and an occasional snowflake came through the smoke hole in the roof. Audrey looked at her father sleeping against his saddle, reaffirming that their decision to search for him had been right. The flames crackled, and she saw that the small pieces of wood had caught.

Looking back at Brad and her father, she saw that they were still asleep. She picked up the empty coffeepot and filled it with water from a canteen. Placing the coffeepot on the rocks at the edge of the fire, she wondered how much it had snowed during the night. She gently pushed back the edge of the canvas tarp and looked outside; the wind was still blowing. Looking to the right, she saw the horses next to the lean-to, sheltered from the wind by a tight clump of rocks and bushes. She was judging how much snow was on the ground when Brad touched her arm.

"Is it still snowing?" he asked.

"Yes, but not as heavy as last night. It looks like we have well over a foot of snow."

"Pa's got to get his strength back," said Brad. "What do we have left to eat?"

"Three cans of beans, a few apples, and half a slab of bacon."

Brad looked at the small stack of wood and said, "As soon as the weather clears, I'll go hunting. Until then I'd better get some more wood."

"Pa's still asleep," said Audrey. She paused before continuing, "I've got water heating for tea, but he needs a good meal."

"When we were riding up on Sunday, I saw some geese going south. They were stragglers though; most of the geese have already gone. I might be lucky, and get one, or maybe even a pheasant. It'll be tough with a rifle. I'm not a marksman like Pa."

"The water's boiling; I'll make some tea. It'll warm you up before you go out for the wood," said Audrey.

She added the tea leaves and moved the pot away from the fire. Brad got their tin mugs and looked through the food bag. "I packed six cans of beans. We only have three left, but we've only eaten one. A slab of bacon, a can of syrup, and a small bag of apples are missing, too."

"I unpacked the horses and put everything in the lean-to," Audrey assured him.

"The bag probably came loose when we raced down

here after we heard the shot or after we shot the wolves," Brad concluded.

"That means the food is somewhere between here and the bottom of that butte, a couple of miles away. We'll never find it under all that snow."

"I'll just have to shoot straight on the first shot," said Brad with a smile. "What's your choice, pheasant, duck, goose, antelope, or deer?"

"Whatever you find, we'll be thankful for," she said, filling his mug with tea.

Brad took a scalding sip and wrapped his hands around the mug. "The tea's pretty good; probably because I'm hungry, cold, scared, and tired; how about you?"

"I'm not scared anymore, but I am hungry, cold, and tired. Pa needs to have that bullet taken out, but I think it's best to let Doc Adams do it. What do you think?"

"I agree. The bleeding's stopped; that's the important thing. We daubed the wound with carbolic acid like Doc Adams does. Good food is what he needs now," Brad said as he lifted the mug of tea to his lips. Finding the tea had cooled to drinking temperature, he emptied the mug in a couple of gulps. He put on his hat, snugged up his coat, and picked up the ax.

"I'll cook some bacon and a couple of cans of beans," said Audrey as her brother left the lean-to.

Brad checked on the horses, and then went to the fallen tree. He wiped away the snow with the blade of the ax and began chopping. A few minutes later, he filled his arm with wood and returned to the lean-to.

"Here's the first load. I'll go get another and then feed the horses," said Brad. A few more minutes of chopping and he had another armload of wood. As he approached the lean-to, Audrey opened the flap.

"I filled the feedbags for the horses," she said. "Pa's stirring, and breakfast will be ready in a minute."

Brad took the feed bags and walked to the horses. Ebony nickered when he slipped the feedbag over her head, as did Blaze. He put a feedbag on Pa's horse and returned to the lean-to.

"Blaze and Ebony nickered when I gave them their bag of oats," said Brad as he lowered the canvas tarp.

"They're still young and probably want to run through the snow," commented his father. "Is it still snowing?"

"It's pretty light now, and the wind is dying down," said Brad. "I'll go hunting after breakfast and try to find some game."

"Take Ebony," advised his father. "You'll tire yourself out slogging through the snow on foot."

Audrey put three tin plates in her lap, turned her head to her father, and said, "Pa?"

He looked at her questioningly, and then realized that she was asking him to say grace. He bowed his head and said, "Lord, thank you bringing us together to share this meal you have placed before us. Please help us wisely use the knowledge you have given us for our return to Riverton. Thank you for guiding Brad and Audrey in their search for me and for delivering us from evil. Amen."

Audrey looked at their father. His eyes were closed as tears ran down his cheeks. Audrey wiped a tear from her own eye, swallowed hard, and sat up straight.

She held out a plate, "Here's your plate, Pa. Beans and bacon are ready."

Brad filled the mugs with tea, and they ate in silence. After they had eaten, Brad asked, "Can you tell us what happened after the holdup, Pa?"

"We rode north for a few miles, then east down a stream about a mile. Duke was laughing about the posse that would come and how they'd never find our tracks. Then we turned south a few miles before finally going east. We stayed at a grove of trees about half a day's ride west of here until Sunday. We camped here until yesterday."

"What made Duke decide to take Lutz and backtrack, Pa?"

"No one knows. He suddenly stood up and said that someone was following us. Told his men to break camp and be ready to leave when he came back. He took Lutz with him and they rode west. When he came back, he said Lutz was right; no one was following him. There was a storm coming, and they'd best get back to their hideout. I heard a couple of his men talking; one said that their hideout was about a half day's ride due east."

"We guessed right," said Brad. "We sat on top of the hill where the stage was held up and ate lunch. We concluded that Duke would go east and that he probably had a small ranch out here."

"We rode about five miles due east from the holdup site, and then north for several miles. That's where we found their tracks," added Audrey.

Brad swallowed some tea and said, "We left Riverton early Sunday morning, reaching the holdup site around noon. We stopped early Sunday evening, caught some fish for supper, and spent the night without a fire. If

Duke Badger was close by, we didn't want him to see our camp fire."

"Wise move," confirmed his father. "Every night, Duke had a couple of men ride out just after dark to look for camp fires."

"Each time we came to the crest of a hill, we'd crawl to the top to scout out what laid ahead. We were afraid we might ride into his camp," said Audrey.

"Running Bear trained you well," said their father.

"We should start riding back in a few hours," suggested Brad. "I'm going hunting for some game. You need to eat a good meal before we leave. We'll try to camp at the same place we were Sunday night. The wind will cover our tracks if Duke comes back to check on you."

Brad refilled the magazine of his rifle with cartridges. "I'll bring Ebony over here to saddle her. No need to struggle through the snow with the blanket and saddle." Brad buttoned up his coat, put on his hat, and pushed aside the flap of the lean-to. In a few minutes, he was back with Ebony. Audrey was waiting for him outside the lean-to.

"Here's the saddle blanket," she said. Brad put the blanket on Ebony. When he turned around, Audrey was behind him with the saddle.

"Thanks," he said, taking the saddle. When he finished saddling Ebony, he turned around and asked, "How's Pa? He seems stronger."

Audrey handed Brad his rifle. "He's asleep again," she said as a tear ran down her face. "Duke didn't let him get much sleep, gave him very little food, took his shoes, and then shot him. He needs food and rest before he travels. And before you say it, yes, I know we should leave as soon as possible."

"An evil monster; Reverend Wesley's description of Duke fits him perfectly," said Brad. "I'll do my best to find some game. Take care of Pa. I'll be back as soon as I can."

Audrey watched her brother ride into the trees. When she could no longer see him, she pulled the canvas tarp back and entered the lean-to. Her father was still asleep. She put another small piece of wood on the fire, filled the coffeepot with water, and then placed it on the rocks in the fire pit.

"Let's stop for a moment, Ebony," whispered Brad, gently pulling back on the reins. "I saw something move in those trees."

Brad looped the reins across his saddle horn and slowly pulled his rifle out of its scabbard. Carefully levering a shell into the chamber, he watched the trees. Again, he saw something move. Brad held the rifle with both hands as he gently touched Ebony's flanks with his heels. Ebony moved forward. A small doe limped out of the trees; she was injured and struggling in the deep snow. There was more movement in the trees. Brad watched closely as two wolves followed her from the clump of trees.

"Whoa," whispered Brad. Ebony stopped; Brad raised his rifle and shot. The crack of the rifle broke the silence of the forest, and a small clutch of birds flew out of the trees. Ebony flinched at the sound but otherwise remained motionless.

"Good girl," soothed Brad.

Harold Benton sat up and looked at Audrey

questioningly. Before either could speak, there was a second shot, and then a third. Audrey reached into her saddlebag and pulled out her father's gunbelt and pistol.

"Pa, we brought your pistol, just in case." Then she pulled her rifle out of its scabbard and pushed back the canvas flap of the lean-to.

Brad put his rifle back into its scabbard and then squeezed Ebony's flanks. When they reached the doe, he stopped, dismounted, and tied his rope around the doe's hind legs. After tying the other end of the rope around his saddle horn, he mounted, reined Ebony back toward the lean-to, and clucked her into a walk.

Audrey saw Brad coming through the trees to the lean-to. When he got closer, she called, "Were those three shots yours?"

"Yes! I got a doe. She was injured, and two wolves were chasing her."

"You got the wolves, too?" asked Audrey.

"I got the first one, but missed the second."

"Brad," giggled Audrey mischievously, "I think you should dress the deer at the tree where we found Pa. You can use his old clothes for rags and to wrap the entrails. Then, when Duke Badger comes to check on Pa, he'll find bloody and shredded clothes around the tree. What do you think?"

Brad's grim face slowly changed to a broad grin. "I like your idea. Duke will believe that the wolves got Pa."

Audrey watched as Brad walked Ebony to the tree where they had found their father. When the doe was under the tree he stopped, dismounted, and untied the rope from his saddle horn. He selected a tree branch about ten feet off the ground and tried to throw the rope across it, succeeding on the second try. Then he took the end of the rope back to Ebony and tied it to the saddle horn. Gently touching Ebony's bridle, he walked her forward. When the doe was a foot off the ground, he stopped.

"Audrey, can you bring the rags!" requested Brad as he began dressing the deer.

Audrey expanded the fire pit away from the lean-to and added some small branches. In a few minutes, she and their father had chunks of venison roasting on sticks over the fire.

"I'm going to saddle the horses while you're cooking," said Brad. "We should be able to leave around mid-morning. I want to get as much distance as possible between Duke Badger and us. He's unpredictable, and may come back to check on Pa. Let's tear down the lean-to and try to wipe out any evidence of our stay. I'll drag the four wolves we shot into the forest. If it snows again, he won't see our tracks or campsite. If it doesn't snow, we need to be well on our way to Riverton."

"I'll cook extra so we can eat without a fire if we have to," said Audrey.

Brad saddled the horses and filled the canteens at the small stream.

"Ready for an early lunch?" asked Audrey, offering Brad a mug of tea. "The venison is ready."

"I'm always ready to eat," he said, and took the mug.

"This venison's good," declared their father, waving the piece of meat.

He'd taken a second stick of venison from the fire when Brad asked, "Pa, how long do you think you can ride before we have to stop?"

"Several hours, maybe more," Mr. Benton replied. "All that sleep and Audrey's cooking has really helped. The wound still hurts, but it's not bleeding."

"Maybe we can make it to our last campsite," suggested Audrey.

"We can try, but with the snow and Pa's wound, we may have to stop sooner," Brad reasoned.

"True, but we won't be stopping at every hill and crawling to the top either," countered his sister.

"We'd best break camp and go while the weather's good," advised their father.

Audrey packed the coffeepot, skillet, mugs, and plates in the saddlebags. Brad cut chunks of raw venison, put it in the empty food bags, and strapped the bags to the back of his saddle. They helped their father onto his horse, and then Brad tore the lean-to apart and scattered the branches among the trees. Audrey scattered the ashes from the fire and threw the fire's rocks toward the stream.

"I'll drag the remains of the doe away from the area," said Brad. "Then, if Duke finds the carcass, he won't connect it with the bloody tree and clothes. Audrey, take the lead and break the trail. I'll follow with the deer's carcass."

Audrey clucked Blaze into a fast walk. Their father was next, followed by Brad. In a few minutes, they were on the plains. Brad stopped, untied the remains of the deer, and remounted Ebony.

"Let's go," he said. "We'll take turns leading, so one

horse won't have to do all the hard work of breaking the trail."

Around noon Audrey asked, "How do you feel, Pa? We've been going a couple of hours."

"I'm very tired," he replied. "I need to stop for a few minutes."

"There's a small stand of trees at the bottom of the swale," stated Brad. "They'll shelter us from the wind, and we can eat some more of that venison."

They stopped in the trees and helped their father dismount. Audrey opened one of her saddlebags, brought out a sack of cooked venison, and passed it around.

"The western sky is dark," observed Brad. "Another snowstorm is coming, but I think we'll be able to make our last campsite before it arrives."

"I don't like the idea of another snowstorm," replied their father, "but I do like that fact that it will hide our tracks if Duke Badger comes to check on my remains."

"He'll find your remains," giggled Audrey with a big smile. "We used the clothes you had on when we found you to wrap the deer's entrails. The wolves will find your clothes and shred them to get to the entrails."

"Did Running Bear teach you that?" asked their father.

"No, but he did teach us to think like the enemy. Duke Badger will probably send someone to look for your remains, and he'll find your shredded clothes. We want him to believe that the blood is yours and that your bones are close by and covered with snow."

Their father pondered Audrey's comments and replied, "Good idea."

"We've got two to three hours of riding before we reach our campsite. Can you make it, Pa?" asked Brad.

"I have to," he replied. "Let's go."

Brad checked the loads on the horses, tightening some of the ties and ropes. After assuring that the loads were secure, they helped their father mount his horse.

"Are you ready, Pa?" asked Brad.

"As ready as I'm going to be; let's go."

Audrey mounted Blaze and took the lead as they headed west to their earlier campsite.

The wind was picking up by the time they reached their old campsite. Brad led them into the cluster of trees above the stream, stopping in the small clearing.

"Stay on your horse, Pa. We'll build the lean-to and fire; then we'll help you down," said Audrey.

Brad used the frame of their previous lean-to to build their new shelter. Audrey took the shovel and cleared the ground. By the time she had cleared away most of the snow, Brad had laid several branches for the roof.

"It looks like it's going to start snowing any minute. I'll get some rocks and dig the fire pit," offered Audrey.

"I tripped over a fallen tree when I got the branches," said Brad. "I'll bring some wood and then finish the lean-to."

Using the axe blade, Brad scraped the snow off the fallen tree. Starting at the top, he quickly chopped an armload of wood and took it inside the lean-to. He returned to the fallen tree and filled his hat with wood chips.

Audrey had completed the fire pit and was adjusting

the rocks for the skillet and coffeepot when Brad arrived with the wood chips.

"These will work as kindling. I'll finish the lean-to while you start the fire."

Nodding toward their father, Audrey said, "Pa's starting to wobble in the saddle. I'll start the fire, get some fir boughs and his blankets."

"Keep an eye on him," Brad advised. "We may have to help him down before you're ready for him."

Audrey arranged the wood chips and some small branches for the fire. "Pa, I'll have the fire going and some blankets for you in a couple of shakes. Can you wait?"

"For a fire and a blanket, I can wait five shakes."

"I'm getting the kerosene and matches now," she said, opening a saddlebag.

Audrey poured a little kerosene on the wood chips and small branches. After carefully putting the cap back on the can, she placed it in the saddlebag and lit a match on the bottom of the skillet. The wood chips and branches were burning down when Brad arrived with another load of branches for the lean-to. He laid the branches down, put a couple of small sticks of wood on the fire, and looked at his father.

"Here are the fir boughs for his bed," said Audrey, setting down an armload of boughs. "As soon as they're in place, we can cover them with a blanket for Pa."

They quickly readied the boughs and blanket before going to their father. Brad grasped the bridle and led their father's horse to the lean-to. "We'll help you down, Pa. Audrey's got the fire going and your bed's ready."

"I'm ready for that," their father replied. "My head's spinning."

Brad and Audrey helped him dismount and walk the few steps to his blanket, easing him down in front of the fire. Audrey helped him sit up while Brad got the saddle and saddle blanket.

"Your saddle is behind you, Pa. Lean back and rest; we'll wake you for dinner," said Audrey.

Audrey covered her father with a blanket and put another piece of wood on the fire. Snow began to fall lightly. Brad left for a third load of branches, and Audrey began unloading the horses. She had finished when Brad returned with his last load of branches for the lean-to.

"Let's put up the canvas tarp," said Brad. "Then I'll get the saddles."

Brad untied the tarp from the back of his horse and brought it to the lean-to. "Hold it up while I do the first tie," instructed, Brad unrolling the tarp.

"The snow is getting heavier," said Audrey. "The wind is starting to pick up, too."

Brad did another tie and predicted, "It's going to be easier than yesterday though."

"Less snow and the wind's not as strong," agreed his sister.

"One more tie and we'll be done, Pa," announced Brad.

Audrey looked at their father. "He's asleep again. I'll close the canvas after I've filled the canteens and coffeepot. Then you can give the horses the last of their oats."

Brad removed the saddles and tethered the horses in the shelter of the lean-to before returning to the fallen tree. He chopped another armload of wood and took it to the lean-to. He stacked it inside and then returned to the fallen tree.

Audrey came back from the stream and set the coffeepot on the rocks at the edge of the fire. Opening her saddlebag, she removed the canvas feedbags and divided the last of the oats equally among them. Picking up the feedbags, she went to the horses and slipped the bags over their heads. Through the falling snow, she watched her brother chopping wood for the fire. Feeling the chill of the wind, she returned to the lean-to, pulled down the canvas, and added a big pinch of tea to the boiling water in the coffeepot.

"Here's the last load of wood," panted Brad, pulling back the canvas. "This should last us until noon tomorrow."

Brad looked around their shelter and saw some snow blowing under the side of the lean-to next to his blanket. "I'd better shovel some more snow along that side to keep the wind out. I'll take the feed bags off the horses, too."

"The tea will be ready by the time you get back," said Audrey. "I'm starting the venison now."

Brad shoveled some more dirt and snow around the base of the lean-to as the storm gradually increased in intensity. When he finished, he leaned exhaustedly on the shovel and looked at the swirling snow. Propping the shovel against the canvas, he slowly trudged through the snow to the horses.

"Ebony, that was the last of the oats," he said removing her feedbag. "After this you'll just have snow covered grass until we get back to Riverton." Ebony nickered and rubbed her head against his shoulder. Brad patted her neck and got the other feedbags before returning to the lean-to.

Audrey heard Brad coming and filled his tin mug with hot tea. "How much snow do you think we'll get?" she asked, handing him the mug.

"Not as much as the last storm," he replied as he took the tea. "But it's already enough to cover our tracks."

Audrey looked at their father and said, "Time to wake him up; supper's just about ready."

Brad sat down on his blanket, turned to his father, and said, "Pa, supper's ready. You have to wake up."

Harold Benton opened his eyes and blinked, "I was dreaming about Duke Badger."

Audrey looked at her father and smiled. "Pa, there must be something better to dream about than Duke Badger."

"Why dream about something better when you can have the real thing," said Brad. "Here's a mug of hot tea."

Audrey passed a stick of venison to her father and then to Brad. "How far do you think we'll go tomorrow?"

"About to the way station," said Brad. "We can't run the horses in the snow; it's too tiring. We're out of oats, too, so the horses will have less stamina. Once we reach the road, though, we may be able to travel faster. If the stage and freight wagons have traveled on the road, they'll make it a lot easier. We may be able to let the horses trot."

"Then we've got to camp at least one more night before we get home," said Audrey as she took another stick of venison from the fire.

"How are you doing, Pa?" asked Brad.

"Much better than when you found me, but I couldn't have gone much further today."

"Are you up to telling us more about Duke?" asked Audrey.

"Only if I can keep eating," said her father. "Or as Brad would say - I'm so hungry, I could eat the hooves off of a horse."

"Did you ride double all the time?" asked Brad.

"No, just a few hours the first day. They had some spare horses in a makeshift corral. If a posse came after them, Duke's gang would have fresh horses, and the posse wouldn't. It was a good plan."

"We caught up with you so fast," said Audrey. "Why did he stay in the area?"

"Each morning, he'd send his men out to setup cross-fire ambushes. If a posse had found their trail, Duke's men would have massacred them. He laughed about being ready to shoot up the posse. Mid-day Sunday, a rider came in and told them that the posse had passed the way station on the way to Riverton. When the rider left, he told us we'd break camp Monday morning."

"Then we were only a half day behind them. It's a good thing we crawled to the top of each rise and didn't have a fire Sunday night," said Audrey.

"Why did he wait to break camp until noon on Monday?" asked Brad.

"His men had been complaining about the early morning rides to set up ambushes for the posse. He let them sleep in and have a leisurely breakfast," said their father, nodding to stay awake.

"Pa, you don't have to keep talking," said Audrey. "Go to sleep. We can talk again tomorrow."

Brad took his father's empty mug and gave it to Audrey. Audrey poured the last of the tea into the mugs.

"Duke is trail smart," conceded Brad. "It's a good thing we crawled to the top of each rise. We must have been within a few miles of him when we stopped Sunday night."

"Yes, and I'm glad we cooked our fish before he stopped for the day," said Audrey. "When he sent his men out in the evening to look for camp fires, ours was out."

"What do we have left for breakfast?" asked Brad.

"We still have some bacon, so I'm going fix the last of the potatoes, bacon, and some venison."

Brad put another piece of wood on the fire and said, "That will leave bacon and venison for Thursday morning. Between here and the last campsite is a bag with the syrup, oats for the horses, canned beans, apples, and a slab of bacon."

"It's buried under the snow, someplace on the prairie," muttered Audrey wryly.

"What is there for Thursday night?" asked Brad.

"Only venison," replied Audrey."

"Then we'll just have venison," confirmed her brother.

Audrey looked at him and smiled, adding, "We have tea to go with the venison."

Brad looked at his sister, saw the smirk on her face, and laughed. "We can't complain. The horses will have nothing but snow covered grass."

Brad poked the fire with a stick and finished his mug of tea. "I knew we'd find Pa; now we just have to get him home. I think we should skirt around the way station. What do you think?"

Audrey thought for a moment and then said, "Since Pa told us about that rider coming out Sunday, I agree."

"The Lord has certainly given us a challenge," lamented Brad. "Pa's wounded, we're out of oats for the horses, and we're up against snow storms, freezing weather, and a spy at the way station."

Audrey laughed. "We've out-smarted Duke Badger so far; we can keep doing it. These new challenges are small compared to what we've already overcome. You've done the heavy work, get some sleep. I'll stay up and watch Pa for a bit. We'll talk more in the morning."

CHAPTER 10
THE SPY IS CAPTURED

Wednesday, 27 October 1880: The morning arrived with sunshine and no wind. The chirping of birds and chattering of squirrels was refreshing after two days of wind and snow. Brad opened his eyes and sat up. Audrey and their father were still asleep. He added some small branches to the fire and thought about breakfast. Filling the coffeepot with water, he carefully used it to push the ashes off the rocks at the edge of the fire.

Harold Benton opened his eyes and watched his son adjusting the coffeepot on the rocks. "Morning, son. Sunshine and no wind should make today easier than yesterday. We can stay at the way station tonight."

"I don't think we should, Pa; Audrey and I talked about that last night. You said a rider came Sunday and told Duke that the posse had passed the way station on their way back to Riverton. We think Duke Badger has someone keeping tabs on way station or watching the way station."

"That's right," agreed Audrey, waking up to the conversation. "If he sees us, especially you, he'll tell Duke and he may even ambush us. We think it's safer going around and camping out another night."

Their father thought for a moment and replied, "You're right. We've made it this far by avoiding trouble. There's no need to invite it when we're almost home."

"The water's boiling," said Brad. "We can have a mug of tea before breakfast."

"Breakfast will be bacon and venison," announced Audrey.

Brad put on his boots, "I'll check the horses."

Harold Benton watched his son push the canvas aside and leave the lean-to. "Audrey, what did your grandmother say about you and Brad coming to search for me?"

Audrey shrugged her shoulders. "She told us that she knew we were going to search for you, no matter what anyone said. We tried to avoid answering her, but she said she could help us plan, even if she couldn't go with us. So, we told what we had planned. She made some good recommendations, such as bringing the kerosene and a complete set of clothes for you. We made a list, and she reviewed it."

Audrey continued telling her father about Nana's help in planning their search. She added a big pinch of tea as she spoke.

"That's Victoria," said her father. "She learned a lot from her husband. He was a scout for General Grant."

"That's what she told us," said Audrey. "She said he was trained by an Indian."

Brad pulled back the canvas and entered the lean-to. "I watered the horses and knocked the snow off the grass for them."

"Have a mug of tea," said Audrey, filling the mugs. "The bacon and venison are already frying. I thought we would save the potatoes for tonight. It's only a few potatoes, but it is something."

"Oh, good, we can eat bacon, potatoes, and venison -again," groaned Brad.

"Audrey was telling me about Victoria and that she knew you two were going to search for me," said their father.

"I didn't know we were so transparent," said Brad. "We didn't say anything, but she just - well, she just knew."

"Reverend Wesley knew too," said Audrey. "He knew even before Nana talked to him about us."

"That's why he's a good reverend," said their father. "He understands how people think. He helps them think clearly and understand what they should do. We're fortunate to have him as our reverend."

"Breakfast is ready," announced Audrey.

Audrey filled their plates with bacon and venison, and they ate hungrily. Brad was the first to speak.

"It's real nice outside. No wind, no snow, and the sun is shining. We should be able to make good time today. I'll saddle the horses as soon as I finish eating."

"I'll cook some more venison for lunch," said Audrey. "It should be ready by the time we break camp."

Brad left the lean-to and a few minutes later returned with the horses. While the venison cooked, Audrey passed the saddles and saddlebags to him as he readied the horses. The rifles were the last things she handed to him.

"One last round of tea," said Audrey. "About a half-mug apiece. I've wrapped our venison for lunch in the cloth sacks like I did yesterday."

"I'll fold the canvas while you fill the canteens," said Brad.

Audrey took the canteens to the stream and filled them while Brad untied and folded the tarp. He was fastening the tarp behind his saddle when Audrey returned with the canteens. They tied two canteens on each horse before turning to their father.

"Ready, Pa?" asked Brad.

"Ready," he said, slowly standing up and using the large boulder to steady himself.

Brad and Audrey helped their father mount his horse. He tightened his sheepskin coat as Brad and Audrey checked the campsite one last time.

"It looks good," said Brad. "Let's get moving."

They mounted their horses and Brad took the lead with Ebony. Their father was next, Audrey taking the rear.

The sun was bright and the air still, making the ride rather pleasant after the two snowstorms. The temperature was above freezing, and the depth of the snow lessened as it melted. Late in the morning, they stopped by a rock outcropping for lunch. Brad and Audrey dismounted.

"How do you feel, Pa," asked Brad as they helped their father dismount.

"Much better than yesterday. My shoulder hurts, and I can't move my arm without a lot of pain, but Doc Adams will fix that."

"Venison for lunch," announced Audrey in an overly

cheerful voice. "This should be a real treat. We usually don't have it twice in one day."

"Then tonight will be a luxury," laughed their father, "because we'll have it three times in one day."

Brad looked to the west and spoke. "Pa, if I were spying on the way station, I'd want to be in the hills above it. I think we ought to turn south a couple of miles before we reach the road. What do you think?"

Their father thought for a moment and said, "I agree. We're making good time and can probably make it to the other side of the way station by late afternoon. There's a hilly area with trees and a spring a few miles southeast of the way station. It'd be a nice place to camp."

"Isn't that Indian Hill, the area that Running Bear told us about?" questioned Audrey. "It's supposed to be haunted by Indians."

"That would be a great place," agreed Brad. "We can camp on the side of the hill. From there we can see miles in every direction."

"Could the spy be living on that hill?" asked Audrey.

"He could be, but he couldn't see the way station from there," replied their father.

"But, could he see the road," confirmed Brad, "right?"

Their father pondered the question for a moment. "I believe that he could see the road about a mile south of the way station."

"Well," suggested Brad, "we can try to skirt Indian Hill, or we can camp on it. What do you think, Audrey?"

"I think we ought to go to Indian Hill," affirmed Audrey with a mischievous gleam in her eye. "If the spy is there, we can capture him and take him back to Riverton. If he's not there, we have an excellent campsite."

"If he is camped there, we can ride right in because he won't be expecting anyone. By the time he recognizes Pa, we'll have the drop on him," said Brad.

"Pa, is that okay with you?" asked Audrey.

"I like the idea; let's do it."

"Ready to mount up?" asked Brad.

Their father pulled his pistol out and handed it to Brad. "Check it out, son. Make sure it's loaded and working properly. Then I'll be ready to go."

Brad examined the pistol closely as he slowly turned the cylinder. He gently pulled back the hammer a little and then eased it back to its resting position. "It looks good, Pa. It's got a cartridge in every chamber, and everything moves freely."

"Help me mount up, and let's go to Indian Hill," said their father, holstering the pistol.

They helped him mount his horse and then started toward Indian Hill. Audrey took the lead this time, followed by their father; Brad was last.

Three hours later, they stopped at a small stream to water the horses. Indian Hill was clearly visible in the distance; they all studied it for a moment.

Brad was the first to speak. "It's about an hour ride from here."

"How do you feel, Pa?" asked Audrey.

"I'm pretty tired, but I can make Indian Hill, especially if we might capture a spy. Let's talk about what we're going to do."

The three of them discussed how to approach Indian Hill. After several minutes, they agreed upon a plan. Brad took the lead, and they started toward Indian Hill. The horses were tired and hungry, and the snow made walking even harder for them. By the time they reached the bottom of the hill, it was late afternoon.

"There's some tracks, Pa," said Brad. "It looks like a horse came this way earlier today. I'll follow them."

The tracks followed an old Indian trail up the hill. After a quarter of an hour, Brad held up his hand, and they stopped. Ahead was a small cabin, a corral, and a large shed. A saddled horse was in the corral, but no smoke was coming out of the chimney. Brad urged Ebony forward and headed to the cabin.

Brad stopped in front of the cabin and shouted, "Anyone home!" There was no response, so he shouted again, "I'm coming in!"

Brad dismounted, leaving his reins looped on his saddle, and approached the door of the cabin. "I'm coming in!" he shouted.

Brad opened the door and looked inside. He saw a man face down on the floor; the stench of liquor permeated the small cabin. Brad backed out the door and waved for his father and Audrey to come.

Audrey trotted Blazed to the cabin, quickly dismounted, and joined Brad at the door of the cabin. She looked at the man snoring on the floor and said, "Let's see what Pa wants us to do."

Audrey and Brad helped their father dismount and enter the cabin. Their father kept his hand close to his pistol as Brad pulled a liquor bottle and a large piece of paper out of the man's right hand. Brad looked at the paper and said, "It's a "Wanted" poster."

Audrey eyed the paper and then the man on the floor. "It looks like him, but I can't be sure. Can you turn him over, Brad?"

"I'll give it a try." Brad grunted as he rolled the man over.

Audrey carefully examined the wanted poster and compared it to the man on the floor. "They're the same. He's the man on the poster, Garth Pugh. He has the flattened nose and a thick jagged scar on the right side of his face. And," she said with a snicker, "he's worth some money. There's a one-thousand-dollar reward for him, dead or alive."

"He's dead drunk," observed their father. "By the looks of things, he started drinking earlier today and passed out. He could wake up and become violent, so be careful. Brad, tie his hands with that rope and run it across the roof beam."

Brad tied Garth's hands with a strip of rawhide and then tied a rope to the rawhide. He threw the rope across the roof beam. Audrey took the end of the rope, pulled out the slack, and tied it to the bunk. Brad unbuckled the man's gunbelt, slowly pulling it free to avoid waking him.

"I'll put his gun in my saddlebag and take care of the horses," offered Brad.

"We'll watch Garth while you're gone," said his father.

Brad unsaddled the horses, including Garth's, and put the saddles in the small barn's tack room while the horses drank at the spring-fed water trough. Almost as an afterthought, he looked around the barn.

Inside the cabin, Audrey picked up some kindling and a sheet of newspaper and said, "I'll start a fire in the stove, Pa."

In a few minutes, the fire was burning and the chill was beginning to leave the room. With night coming,

Audrey lit a kerosene lantern and noticed a bag in the corner of the room.

"What's in the bag?" asked her father.

"Food!" she exclaimed. "Bacon, beans, apples, potatoes, flour, cream of tartar, baking soda, syrup, and even some canned peaches."

Brad came in the door with the saddlebags over his shoulder and the rifles in his hands. "There's a big sack of oats in the barn, so I fed the horses. His horse was real hungry; she acted like she hadn't been fed for a couple of days."

"I'm sure you didn't over feed her," responded his father looking at his son. "We don't want the horse to founder." Brad shook his head in response.

"We're having beans and potatoes with our venison tonight," said Audrey. "There are even canned peaches for dessert."

"It'll be dark in a little bit," observed Brad. "I'll fill the canteens and coffeepot."

"Make that two coffeepots," suggested Audrey. "Garth has some coffee in his bag of food."

Brad returned with the coffeepots and canteens full of water. The smell of sizzling bacon filled the small cabin as he put the two coffeepots on the stove. Brad looked at Garth and said, "I'd better tie his feet while he's still out."

"Dinner will be ready shortly," announced Audrey.

Brad set the plates, knives, forks, and spoons on the table. He had just finished when Garth groaned and turned over.

"He'll be awake in a few minutes," warned their father. "Stand back, just in case he gets violent."

Brad and Audrey moved the small table away from the man and waited.

"Audrey, did you put that wanted poster in your jacket?" asked Brad.

"Of course," she said.

Garth groaned, shook his head, and started to stand up. He fumbled and then realized that his hands and feet were tied. "What the?" he snorted.

"There'll be no vulgar language, Mr. Pugh. There is a lady present," ordered Harold Benton.

Garth looked around the room, first at Brad, then at Audrey, and finally at Harold Benton's pistol.

"How'd ya know my name?" he asked.

"Very simple," said Brad. "It's on your wanted poster."

"If you'd like some coffee, I'll pour you a cup," offered Audrey. "It should help your headache."

Garth looked at Audrey, his tied hands, and then again Audrey. "How'd ya know my head aches?"

"Anyone who'd drink a whole bottle of whiskey in one sitting has to have a headache."

"Ya, I'd like some coffee."

"I unsaddled and fed your horse," said Brad. "She was real hungry. You must have forgotten to feed her yesterday."

Audrey poured Garth a cup of coffee and placed it on the floor in front of him.

Garth looked at Audrey, then at Harold Benton and asked, "You tie me up, give me coffee, and feed my horse. You know my name from a wanted poster. Whada'ya want?"

"The poster says you're wanted, dead or alive," stated Harold. "What did you do?"

116

"I shot a guy, but he drew first."

"I know how that is, I've shot men too," said Harold.

"You're wanted too?" asked Garth.

"No."

Audrey interrupted before Garth could ask another question. "Would you like some food?" she asked. "I've fried some bacon, venison, and potatoes. There's also a pot of beans."

"Yeah, uh, thanks," replied Garth.

Audrey nodded, and Harold Benton said grace. She served the plates and Brad passed a plate to his father and then to Garth. After Audrey served her own plate, they began eating. Garth looked puzzled as he watched the Bentons.

"Nice food, Audrey," said her father.

"Yes, it's very good," agreed Brad.

"Uh, yeah, the food's good," muttered Garth as he ate awkwardly with his hands tied together.

"Mr. Pugh, what are you doing up here all alone?" asked Brad.

"I'm prospecting for silver."

"I didn't know there was silver in this area. Isn't Leadville the big silver area?" responded their father.

"Yeah, but I thought I'd try this area."

"Your hands aren't callused," observed Audrey. "You must have just started prospecting."

"Uh, right," said Garth looking at his three captors.

"What made you decide to start prospecting in the winter?" asked their father.

"Why all the questions; who are you?" demanded Garth.

"Well," replied Brad, "you haven't told us the truth, so we're asking questions."

"Just be honest," said Audrey.

Garth looked at Audrey, then Brad, and finally at their father.

"I'm waiting," said Harold Benton.

"I'm paid to talk to the folks at the way station, see who's passing through. Local news, and that kind of stuff," explained Garth.

"That sounds like a nice job," said Brad. "Who wants to know about the local news?"

"Uh, a rancher," replied Garth. "His ranch is about a day's ride from here."

"What's the rancher's name?" asked Audrey. "How many head of cattle does he have?"

"Why are you asking me these questions?" complained Garth, looking furtively at each of the Bentons.

"We'd like to know the name of the rancher," said Brad.

"I can't tell you his name; he made me promise not to tell anyone."

"Does the name Duke sound familiar?" asked their father.

Garth's eyes opened wide with fear. "Who told you it was Duke Badger?"

"You did," said Brad.

"It's getting late," announced their father, much to Garth's relief. "It's also time to get some sleep since we'll be leaving early tomorrow morning."

"I'll fix up your bed, Pa," said Brad.

Brad went outside and in a few minutes brought in an armload of fir boughs to put under his father's blanket. Then he did the same for Audrey and himself. While Brad was fixing their beds, Audrey cleaned the skillet and dishes. Garth watched in disbelief at the efficiency of Brad and Audrey doing the chores.

Brad hung a kerosene lamp between the stove and Garth's bunk. This would keep Garth in the light so the Bentons could see him. With the light in Garth's eyes and the Bentons in the shadows, Garth wouldn't be able to see them easily.

"Brad, help Garth into his bunk," said his father. "Tie him securely, but make sure he's comfortable."

"Yes, Pa."

Brad helped Garth to his bunk, adjusted his pillow and blankets, and then securely tied his feet to the foot of the bunk. Brad ran a rope through the rawhide tying Garth's hands and tied it to the sides of the bunk, thus allowing his hands some freedom of movement. By the time Brad had finished securing Garth, his father was asleep.

"I'll take the first watch," whispered Audrey. "It'll be below freezing tonight."

"Wake me in a few hours, and I'll take the next watch," whispered Brad in response.

CHAPTER 11
THE SPY GETS A GUN

Thursday, 28 October 1880: Harold Benton slowly pushed the blanket aside and sat up. Darkness filled the cabin, but the sun would rise in a few minutes. He slowly stood up and went to the stove. Using his good arm, he removed the top plate and inserted two sticks of wood into the smoldering embers. Next, he poured water from the jug into Garth's coffeepot, added a fistful of coffee to it, and set it on the back of the stove to heat. By the time he'd filled Brad and Audrey's coffeepot with water, the wood was burning nicely, and the room was warming.

"Brad," said his father softly, "Time to get up. I've got the tea water heating."

Brad sat up, looked at his father, pulled on his boots, and said, "I'll get the horses ready."

"Audrey," whispered her father softly as he gently touched her shoulder, "Time to get up. The tea water is boiling."

Audrey sat up and put on her boots. "Where's Brad?" she asked as she took the other coffeepot of boiling water off the stove and put a big pinch of tea in it.

"He's getting the horses ready. He'll be back by the
120

time breakfast is ready. When he brings the horses, I'll go outside and talk with him."

"Bacon and pancakes for breakfast, Pa," said Audrey, lighting a lantern. "They won't be like Ma's, but they won't be army pancakes either."

Brad finished saddling the horses, put a big scoop of oats in their feedbags, and led them to the cabin. He tethered them to the hitching rail and then slipped the feedbags over their heads.

"Breakfast is just about ready, son," said his father, walking to the hitching rail. Then, in a very soft voice, his father continued, "Garth is a desperate man and will probably try to escape. He is a killer, so don't take any chances. If he gets a gun, don't hesitate to shoot him. If you don't, he'll kill all of us while you're hesitating.

"I don't think I can shoot a man, Pa," stammered Brad.

"I know, and I hope you don't have to. Remember that if you do, you'll be saving our lives. He is no different than the wolves you shot. We must keep him tied at all times to prevent him from escaping. Also, don't get close to him unless I'm close by."

"I understand, Pa," acknowledged Brad.

Brad and his father entered the cabin. Audrey was still cooking pancakes, so Brad tied the tarps, blankets, and supplies on the horses. By the time he'd finished, Audrey had breakfast ready. Brad untied Garth from the bunk while his father kept a watchful eye and his pistol drawn and pointed at Garth.

When they were seated at the table, Audrey nodded to her father.

Brad and Audrey bowed their heads and their father

said grace. Garth looked at his captors in disbelief during Harold Benton's short prayer, but said nothing.

"Here's your plate, Pa, and yours, Mr. Pugh," said Brad as he put the plates of food in front of them.

Audrey poured coffee for her father and Garth as Brad poured tea for his sister and himself.

"Excellent cooking, Audrey," complimented her father. "Victoria and your mother are good teachers, and you've been a good student."

"Yeah," murmured Garth, "Your cookin' is real good."

"Thank you, Mr. Pugh," she replied.

When they finished breakfast, Audrey cleaned the skillet and metal dishes and then packed them in the saddlebags. She had cooked extra bacon and venison, which she wrapped in a cloth sack for later that morning.

"We're ready to mount up," announced Brad.

"Untie his feet, Brad," directed his father as he drew his pistol.

Brad untied Garth's feet and coiled the rope as his father motioned with the pistol for Garth to leave the cabin. Garth mounted his horse and watched as Brad tied his hands to the saddle horn and then tied his feet to each other under the horse's belly. Brad and Audrey helped their father mount up. As Audrey mounted Blaze, Brad tied a long lead to the reins of Garth's horse, and then mounted Ebony.

"Take the lead, son," said their father. "Audrey will follow me."

They rode single file down Indian Hill. Once out of the trees, Brad headed south by southwest until he reached the road to Riverton. Once on the road, they rode two abreast. Garth rode to Brad's left with their father directly behind Garth and Audrey behind Brad. The road had been traveled the previous day and the snow had melted enough so that the horses could trot. In a couple of hours, they reached the stream where Brad had watered the stage horses after the robbery.

Brad reined Ebony to a halt and said, "Let's water the horses and rest for a few minutes."

Audrey looked at her father and asked, "How are you feeling, Pa? Would you like some venison?"

"I'm ready for a nice hot bath," he said, reaching into his pocket for his kerchief.

Harold Benton reached up to wipe his forehead, and in the process, knocked his hat into the stream.

"I'll get if for you, Pa," offered Brad.

Brad dropped the lead rope to Garth's horse, and clucked Ebony into the stream toward the hat. Garth's horse was startled by Brad's action and moved against Harold Benton's horse. Garth took the opportunity to reach for Harold Benton's pistol.

"Audrey!" shouted her father.

Audrey saw Garth struggling with her father and spurred Ebony toward them. She pulled her rifle clear of its scabbard as her father fell from his horse. Although his hands were still tied together, Garth had freed them from the saddle horn and was turning toward Audrey. She saw the pistol in his hand and knew that in a second he would begin shooting. She was too close to shoot with her rifle, the end of the barrel being on the other side of Garth. Summoning all of her strength, she stood up in the stirrups and at the same time brought her rifle barrel straight up. The barrel caught Garth in the chin. There was a sickening crack of breaking bone as the barrel smashed his jaw. Garth emitted a groan and slumped forward in the saddle, unconscious.

"Pa! Are you hurt?" exclaimed Audrey.

"Pa! Audrey! What happened?" shouted Brad.

Audrey leapt off of Blaze with her rifle, picked up the pistol, and rushed to her father who was hanging from his horse by his right foot. She freed his foot from the stirrup and looked at his pale face.

"Pa!" she cried, grasping his shoulders. "Talk to me. Are you all right?"

"Audrey! Is he hurt?" asked Brad, running toward them with his rifle and his father's hat.

"Tie Garth to his saddle," gasped their father. "He got his hands free."

"I'll take care of Garth," vowed Brad angrily.

Brad went back to Ebony, put his rifle in its scabbard, took some rawhide strips off his saddle, and strode quickly to their prisoner. Garth was beginning to regain consciousness and moaned from the pain of his broken jaw. Brad again tied his hands to the saddle horn. Going to Blaze, he took Audrey's rope and looped it around Garth a couple of times, firmly binding his arms to his sides. He took the rest of the rope and wrapped it around his legs and the saddle.

Audrey unbuttoned her father's jacket and shirt to check his wound. "Brad, Pa's bleeding again. Bring the medicine bag."

Brad brought the bag and they daubed the wound with carbolic acid and applied a new dressing.

"Pa, can you make it to Riverton?" asked Brad.

"I have to," he replied. "Help me back onto my horse."

Brad and Audrey helped their father mount his horse. Picking up the lead to Garth's horse, Brad mounted Ebony and headed back to the road. Audrey and their father followed. Garth moaned in pain from his broken jaw, worsened by the movement of the horse.

"Garth is going to bellow all the way to Riverton," predicted Audrey. "Let's give him some laudanum to ease the pain."

"After what he did to Pa, let him suffer," yelled Brad angrily.

"I know how you feel," conceded Audrey. "But we mustn't let our anger make us evil like him."

Brad thought a moment, his face red with anger. He looked at his sister and then at Garth.

"You're right. He'll be in pain for weeks even after he sees Doc Adams," said Brad, halting his horse.

"Wait till he finds out that his jaw was broken by a girl," giggled his sister. "That will hurt worse than the broken jaw."

Brad opened their medical bag and took out the bottle of laudanum. "Audrey, you really know how to hurt a man. I'm glad you're on my side."

Brad remounted and then sidestepped Ebony to Garth's horse. "Garth, this is laudanum. Swallow some to ease the pain."

Garth nodded slowly and Brad stuck the bottle in the side of his mouth, and poured in a little laudanum. Because of his broken jaw, Garth had trouble closing his mouth, letting much of the medicine run down his face. Brad put the bottle in Garth's mouth again, and this time holding Garth's lips shut, raised the bottle for a second time. Garth swallowed twice and Brad removed the bottle, recorked it, and placed it back in the medicine bag.

"Pa, do you need some laudanum?" asked Brad.

"No, let's ride," said his father.

"We'll be in Riverton around noon," said Brad as he squeezed Ebony to a fast trot.

"There's our house," observed Audrey as they trotted past the rutted lane to their home.

"Just a few more minutes, Pa," encouraged Brad. "We're almost in Riverton. I can see the church and the general store."

They remained at a trot as they entered Riverton, slowing down just before they reached the doctor's office. Brad reined Ebony to a halt and jumped off his horse.

"Watch Pa," said Brad, dropping his reins over the hitching rail.

Brad ran across the boardwalk and took the stairs two at a time to Doc Adams' second floor office.

"Mrs. Adams," blurted Brad bursting into the office. "Pa's out front, he's been shot."

"Brad!" exclaimed Mrs. Adams. "You found your father. Bring him right up; I'll get ready for him."

Brad ran down the stairs to get his father. Audrey had dismounted and was tying the horses to the hitching rail when Brad returned.

"Mrs. Adams is getting ready for you now, Pa. Audrey and I'll help you down."

Brad and Audrey helped their father dismount.
126

With their father between them, they helped him up to the boardwalk.

"Brad, Audrey!" boomed Sheriff Tate. "What's going on?"

"Pa's been shot. Please help us get him up to Doc Adams," implored Audrey.

"Hold the door, Audrey. I'll help Brad."

"I'm going now," replied Audrey as she ran up the steps.

"I'm going to pass out, Richard," warned Harold Benton, his knees buckling.

Sheriff Tate caught him, put him over his shoulder, and quickly went up the stairs with Brad following. Audrey held the door open as the sheriff carried in their father. Doc Adams had the table ready, and his wife was already heating water.

"He's in your hands, Ben," said the sheriff, laying Harold on the table.

"I'll do my best," replied the doctor. "Brad, please tell Revered Wesley I need him right away."

"Yes sir," replied Brad running out the door.

The sheriff turned to Audrey and asked, "Who's that fellow you have tied up out front?"

"That's Garth Pugh. He's a spy for Duke Badger. He told Duke when you returned to Riverton with the posse."

"Garth Pugh," said the sheriff thoughtfully, "I think I've seen his name before."

Audrey reached into her coat. "You have; I have a copy of his wanted poster."

Sheriff Tate looked into Audrey's eyes, put his hands on her shoulders, and said consolingly, "Reverend

Wesley told me that you and your brother had gone to search for your father. We prayed for you to succeed, and you did. Let's put Garth in jail; then I'd like you and your brother to tell me about your search."

"Audrey!" exclaimed the reverend, entering Doc Adams' office. "You found your father. I was just about to enter the sheriff's office when I saw Brad. How is he?"

"Duke shot him," sobbed Audrey, throwing her arms around the reverend. "He shot him, took his boots, and left him for the wolves."

"In here, Bob," requested the doctor. "I need your help with Harold, right now!"

"Audrey, Brad, please don't leave," said Reverend Wesley. "Wait here for me."

"We'll be in my office, Reverend," said the sheriff. "We have a prisoner to take care of."

"Pa warned us about him, and he was right," said Brad as they started down the steps.

Sheriff Tate looked at Garth Pugh slumped in his saddle; his face looked grotesque with his bloodied and swollen jaw. "What happened to him?"

"We stopped to rest the horses a couple of hours north of town," said Audrey. "He hurt Pa and grabbed his pistol. I pulled my rifle, but I was too close to shoot him. He was turning to shoot me, and . . ." Audrey choked back a sob and continued, "so I hit him in the jaw with my rifle barrel."

"The fall caused Pa's wound to start bleeding again," added Brad. "We re-bandaged it, and I tied Garth to his horse, real tight."

"I can see that," laughed the sheriff. "Untie his feet

and we'll put him in a cell until Doc Adams can look at him."

"Who in tarnation hog-tied that critter?" hooted Jake Jackson, looking down from the boardwalk.

"My future deputies," replied the sheriff.

"Brad, Audrey, you're back!" exclaimed Jake.

"We found Pa," said Brad. "He's upstairs with Doc Adams."

"Ya found yer Pa!" whooped Jake. "Our prayers were answered."

"I could sure use your help, Jake," said the sheriff. "Help me put this weasel in jail. Then get a buggy and bring Abby to the doc's office so she can see her husband."

Garth was still groggy from the laudanum and didn't understand what was happening as Sheriff Tate and Jake Jackson took him off his horse. Garth staggered and stumbled as they helped him onto the boardwalk, through the front door of the sheriff's office, and into an empty jail cell.

"I'll fetch Abby 'n be right back, Sheriff," declared Jake, mounting Garth's horse and reining it toward the livery.

"Let's go see if Doc Adams is through with your father," suggested the sheriff.

They climbed the stairs and entered Doc Adams' office. Mrs. Adams and the reverend came out of the back room and closed the door.

"Brad, Audrey. My husband got the slug," explained Mrs. Adams. Your father's resting and can go home tomorrow."

"Jake's getting a buggy to pick up their mother," the sheriff told her.

"Who was that man you had hog-tied to the horse?" asked Reverend Wesley.

"Garth Pugh," replied Brad. "He's a spy for Duke Badger."

"How did his face get so messed up and bloodied?"

"I broke his jaw," replied Audrey softly.

"She saved our lives," added Brad. "Garth was going to kill us." Brad and Audrey described Garth's escape attempt. Mrs. Adams and Reverend Wesley listened attentively. When Audrey said that Garth's real pain would come when he found out a girl had broken his jaw, Reverend Wesley laughed.

"I told her that I'm glad she's on my side," remarked Brad as the laughter subsided.

Jake stopped the buggy in front of the sheriff's office and helped Abby Benton down. As soon as her feet touched the boardwalk, she hitched up her long dress and raced up the stairs with Jake lagging behind.

"Audrey, Brad," cried their mother tearfully as she entered the doctor's office, "you brought your father home."

"Ma," sobbed Audrey, hugging her mother. "Duke shot Pa, but we found him just before the wolves got him."

Abby put her arms around Brad and Audrey and looked at Mrs. Adams. With a quivering voice she asked, "Can I see Harold now?"

"Yes," said Mrs. Adams, opening the door to the back room. "He's been asking for you."

Abby saw her husband lying on the bed with a

couple of pillows behind his back to elevate his chest. He slowly turned his head and looked at his tearful wife standing in the doorway, the sun glinting off her golden hair.

"Abby," he whispered. "Brad and Audrey found me."

Reverend Wesley put his hand on the doorknob and said, "Abby, I'll take your children home to Victoria."

"Thank you, Reverend," she said, choking back a sob.

Reverend Wesley put his arms around Brad and Audrey and explained, "They need some time alone. Let's go see Victoria. Jake will bring your mother home."

Brad and Audrey mounted their horses, and Reverend Wesley rode their father's horse. Brad reined Ebony north, starting at a walk. As soon as they were out of town, they broke into a fast trot. A few minutes later they headed down the rutted lane to their house, smoke curling lazily from its chimney.

"Nana must be cooking," said Brad.

"Brad," admonished his sister, "All you ever think about is food."

"After all that venison, wouldn't you like a big piece of apple-blackberry pie?" asked Brad.

"Well," laughed Audrey, "that's different."

"You grandmother's apple-blackberry pie is superb," confirmed the reverend.

Brad and Reverend Wesley unsaddled the horses while Audrey put a scoop of oats in their feed troughs. She and the reverend waited while Brad climbed up to the hayloft and forked some hay down for the horses.

Brad looked at the blankets, tarp, saddlebags, and other equipment and said, "I'll come unpack later. Let's just go in the house."

They left the barn and went to the front door of the house. Brad opened the front door and motioned Audrey and the reverend to enter. They heard their grandmother in the kitchen singing.

"Nana," announced Audrey, "we're home. Reverend Wesley's with us."

"Brad! Audrey!" Victoria rushed from the kitchen and put her arms around them.

"We found Pa," proclaimed Brad. "He's at Doc Adams'. He can come home tomorrow."

"Ma's with him now," added Audrey. "Jake Jackson will bring her home in a buggy."

"Victoria," announced Reverend Wesley, "good triumphed over evil."

Victoria fought to hold back her tears and whispered, "Yes, it did."

"With the help of your grandchildren, evil lost this battle," stated the reverend.

Victoria smiled, looked at her two grandchildren, and said, "If you're hungry, I have an apple-blackberry pie that's just cooled off. Would you like some?"

"Yes!" exclaimed Brad.

"He's tired of bacon and venison, and so am I," sighed Audrey.

"Reverend?" queried Victoria.

"Most assuredly," he said. "Your pies are superb."

"We'll wash-up and help you," offered Audrey.

"You'll do no such thing," Victoria said in mock

indignation. "Wash-up and have a seat. I'll do the serving."

Brad, Audrey, and Reverend Wesley washed their hands and rinsed their faces at the kitchen pump. Audrey filled two cups with hot coffee for Nana and the reverend while Brad filled two glasses with milk.

"Now," their grandmother said as she put a large piece of pie in front of everyone, "tell me how you found your father, and don't leave out any details. I want to hear it all."

"We skirted west around the way station and stopped for lunch where the stage was held up," said Brad. "We didn't want anyone to know that we were looking for Pa."

"And it's a good thing we did, too," added Audrey. "Duke Badger had a spy watching the way station. We'll tell you more about that later."

Brad continued, "We rode to the top of the hill and ate our lunch."

"We thought that Duke would head east," explained Audrey, "and he did. We hunted for his tracks like Running Bear taught us and found his trail right away."

"So, Running Bear taught you to think like the person you track," interjected the reverend.

"Yes, and it proved to be right," confirmed Audrey.

"We followed his tracks, but each time we came to a rise, we stopped. I'd crawl to the top to see if Duke was just ahead," said Brad.

"We stopped early Sunday night and had a dry camp when it got dark," added Audrey.

"No campfire?" questioned the reverend.

"We had a small one for supper, late in the afternoon,"

answered Audrey, "but we put it out before dark. If Duke Badger looked for a campfire, we didn't want him to see ours."

"We saw some smoke around noon the next day," said Brad. "I climbed to the top of a butte; I saw Duke's camp and some men riding our way."

Audrey swallowed a bite of pie and said, "I found a large cave for us to hide in."

"Lutz looked right at me," said Brad, "but he couldn't see me because it was dark in the cave." Brad paused and looked at his grandmother. "May I have another piece of pie, please?"

"Certainly," she said, going to the kitchen and cutting another piece. "Now continue telling us what happened."

Brad ate, and Audrey continued with their story. "After Duke and Lutz left, we heard a shot and rode to the top of a hill overlooking the camp. We saw Pa with his back to a tree, a stick in his right hand, and," Audrey choked back a sob, "and some wolves were getting ready to attack him."

Reverend Wesley handed Audrey his handkerchief to wipe her tears away. Their grandmother's mouth was open in disbelief at what she was hearing.

Brad looked at his sister and continued telling the story. "I started shooting the wolves on his left, and Audrey shot the wolves to his right. We got four, and the others ran."

"How far away were you?" asked the reverend.

"About 250 yards; it was a long distance for us. I was afraid I might hit Pa, but Audrey said to do what Pa had taught us."

Audrey handed the handkerchief back to the reverend and picked up the story. "Duke had taken Pa's shoes, shot him, and - and left him for the wolves."

Tears started streaming down Audrey's face again and Reverend Wesley handed his handkerchief back to her. Victoria bit her lower lip, pulled a handkerchief out of her pocket, and wiped away her own tears.

Brad continued, "The snow was coming down; it was cold. We bandaged his wound and helped him into the extra clothes we had brought."

"Brad built a lean-to, and I dug a small fire pit," said Audrey."

"We built a small fire in the lean-to for cooking and heat," explained Brad. "Pa would wake up, eat, talk for a few minutes, and then go to sleep again."

"How did Garth get involved?" asked the reverend.

"Pa told us Duke had a man that spied on the way station," said Audrey. "We followed Garth's trail to a cabin on Indian Hill, but he was so drunk he didn't know we were there."

"We had lost two sacks of food, so we were down to just venison," said Brad.

"Now I know why Brad is on his third piece of pie," chuckled their grandmother.

"How did you know Garth was wanted?" asked Reverend Wesley.

"He had his wanted poster," explained Audrey.

"When we stopped to water the horses, he got his hands free and tried to escape," said Brad. "That's when Audrey broke his jaw."

Victoria looked questioningly at Audrey and asked, "How did you break his jaw?"

"He was so close I couldn't shoot, so I just hit him in the jaw with my rifle barrel."

"She knocked him out, too," proclaimed Brad.

"I hear a buggy," said Victoria. "That must be Jake and Abby.

Jake halted the buggy near the oak tree and looped the reins over the hitching post. "Mrs. Benton," he said as he helped her down from the buggy, "ya kin be right proud of yer two young'uns."

"I am, Jake, and so is their father."

"I'll git the reverend and be on m'way. The Missus is holdin' lunch fer me."

Brad, Audrey, Victoria, and Reverend Wesley came to the front porch to greet Abby.

"Abby, I'm so happy that they found Harold," said Victoria. "How is he doing? What did the doctor say?"

"He's weak, tired, and hungry. And," she said hugging Brad and Audrey. "He is also very proud of his two courageous children. They saved him from certain death. He can probably come home tomorrow."

"We'll take good care of him," said Victoria.

"I've got a new family to call on this afternoon," said Reverend Wesley. "I'll see you tomorrow when Jake and I bring Harold home."

CHAPTER 12
HENRY BENTON, U.S. MARSHAL

Saturday, 30 October 1880: Sheriff Tate opened the door leading to his four jail cells. Garth was sitting on the edge of his bunk, his head wrapped in a bandage that held his broken jaw, his forehead resting in his hands.

"Morning Garth, it's Saturday and time see Doc Adams again about your jaw," said the sheriff.

Garth groaned, stood up, and extended his hands for the cuffs that the sheriff held. The sheriff cuffed one hand, Garth turned around, and the sheriff cuffed the other hand.

"Hope ya don't meet that girl again, Garth," taunted a man in another cell. "She might whup ya like she did before."

"Shaddup," growled Garth through his bandaged jaw.

Sheriff Tate unlocked the cell door, and Garth stopped in front of the taunter's cell, his face red with anger, and growled through his teeth, "If I didn't have these cuffs on, I'd break your jaw."

"Let's go Garth. We don't want to keep the good doctor waiting."

The sheriff led Garth out of the jail and onto the

137

boardwalk. Garth stopped, squinting as his eyes adjusted to the bright sunlight.

"Gotta stop," moaned Garth. "I can't see."

The sheriff paused a moment, then Garth started climbing up the stairs. Mrs. Adams held the door open as they entered.

"Have a seat," said the doctor. "It's been two days; let me have a look." He examined the jaw, gently touching Garth's cheek and throat.

"Oooooh," moaned Garth.

"It seems to be healing nicely. Would you like some more laudanum for the pain?" asked Doc Adams.

"Yes," mumbled Garth.

"I'll give you a little, but no more. We've learned that laudanum certainly stops the pain, but it is also very addictive. Keep drinking your milk and mashed vegetables. You'll be up to mashed pancakes in a few weeks."

Sheriff Tate and Garth went down the steps, turned left, and entered the sheriff's office. As they entered, a man stopped in front, dismounted, and followed them in.

"Morning, Sheriff. My name's Henry Benton, Special U.S. Marshal," he said, showing Sheriff Tate his badge. "I'd like to talk to you when you finish with your prisoner."

"Henry Benton," declared the sheriff, "You must be Harold Benton's brother."

"That's right. I'm two years younger."

"I'd appreciate it if you'd help me with this prisoner," said the sheriff. "He's had a real rough time."

"Looks like it," replied Marshal Benton.

Henry helped Sheriff Tate return Garth to his cell. Once the cell door was locked, Garth turned his back to the cell door, and Sheriff Tate removed the handcuffs. Taking the handcuffs, the sheriff returned to his office. Henry Benton followed and shut the door.

"What can I do for you, Marshal?" asked the sheriff.

"I've been assigned to bring in the Badger Gang," said Henry. "What can you tell me about them?"

"I think you have come to the right place," laughed the sheriff. "Garth Pugh, the prisoner you helped me with, is a member of the gang. Audrey Benton broke his jaw, but that's a story I'll let Audrey tell you."

"Audrey Benton? Harold's little daughter?" asked Henry incredulously.

"That's right," replied the sheriff, "Audrey, Harold's not-so-little daughter. She's as tall as her mother. For information about the Badger Gang, you need to talk to your brother and his two children."

"How did they get involved with the Badger Gang?"

"I'll make the story very short," said the sheriff. "Duke Badger held up the stage they were riding, shot the driver, and took your brother captive. Brad and Audrey brought the stage back to Riverton. I took a posse and searched for your brother but didn't find him. Brad and Audrey left the day after I got back, tracked the gang, and found their father. On the way back to Riverton, they captured Garth. They brought him right outside my front door, tied up like an Egyptian mummy. Harold's at home recuperating from a gunshot wound."

"Is he going to be all right?"

"Doc Adams said he's healing well. He'll be able to work half-days starting next week."

"Well I'll be," exclaimed Henry shaking he head. "My own brother spent a week with Duke Badger."

"Brad and Audrey know quite a bit about Duke," said the sheriff. "Duke came within fifteen feet of them, but didn't see them. That was just before they found their father."

"Do you know a good tracker that I can hire to help track the Badger Gang?" asked Henry.

Sheriff Tate smiled, "There are three excellent trackers in the area. Brad and Audrey are two of them. The third is their teacher, Running Bear."

"Where can I find Running Bear?" asked Henry.

"Right here tomorrow morning, a little after nine. He'll be on the nine o'clock train from St. Louis; should be in my office about a quarter-past, and again after the ten o'clock service," said the sheriff.

"I think I'll go see my brother," concluded Henry Benton shaking his head in disbelief. "It appears he has the most information. How do I get to his place?"

"Take the road north," directed the sheriff. "He's about a mile out of town, on the right. It's a large, white, two-story house with a big oak tree in front."

Henry opened the door and said, "I'll talk to you again, maybe before church tomorrow."

Marshal Benton mounted the horse he'd rented at the livery and headed north. In a few minutes, he saw the house that Sheriff Tate had described and turned down the rutted lane leading to it. He dismounted, looped his reins through the hitching post by the oak tree, and walked to the front door.

Victoria was reading in the parlor when she heard

footsteps on the front porch followed by a knock. "I'll get it," she said as she got up and went to the front door.

"Victoria!" exclaimed Henry. "I haven't seen you since the wedding."

"Henry," she squealed, "what brings you to Riverton?"

"I came to see Harold. Sheriff Tate told me about Duke Badger shooting him. How's he doing?"

"He and Abby are upstairs. Abby is sewing, and Harold's reading a book, *20,000 Leagues Under the Sea* by that new French author, Jules Verne. Go up and surprise them. I'll be serving lunch in an hour. Brad and Audrey haven't seen you in years, and they should be back shortly. I hope you have a good appetite."

"Victoria, I always have a good appetite for your cooking."

Henry Benton climbed the stairs and stopped when he got to the top. He listened a moment, and then went to the room where he heard his brother talking. He stood in the doorway and listened as Harold read a passage of the book to Abby.

Harold looked up, saw his brother, and whooped, "Henry! Come in and have a seat."

"Abby, Harold," Henry said as he entered the room. "Before you ask what I'm doing in Riverton, I'll tell you. I'm a Special U.S. Marshal assigned to bring in Duke Badger. Sheriff Tate told me that you, Brad, and Audrey know more about Duke than anyone else."

"That's probably true," agreed Harold Benton.

"Brad and Audrey will be back shortly," said Abby, setting down her sewing. "They're also experts on the Badger Gang."

"How's the book?" asked Henry.

"It's a fascinating book, but it's in French."

"Why not the English translation?" asked Henry.

"David Acker, owner of the Riverton Hotel, brought the book over yesterday. He said since I knew French, I should read the complete French version, not the shorter, English version, which is inaccurate."

"It is a beautiful book with that red and gold cloth binding," replied Henry.

"It has two maps and over a hundred illustrations," described Harold. "He depicts ships and sea creatures in great detail. It is a fascinating novel."

"He reads passages to me in French," said Abby. "He hasn't had time or the opportunity to speak French for years, but that's enough talk about that sea novel for now. I'll let you two discuss Duke Badger while I help Victoria with lunch."

"Reading to your wife in French; that sounds romantic," teased Henry giving Abby a wink as she stood up.

Abby kissed Harold's cheek and gave Henry a brief hug. "It's good to see you again, Henry. Victoria's making beef stew for lunch. We need to get some meat back on your brother's bones."

"He does look a might gaunt," admitted Henry. "I'll do half the talking so he won't get too tired."

Abby left the room and went down the stairs to the kitchen. Henry waited until her footsteps had faded before turning to his brother.

"Sheriff Tate told me Duke took you as a captive," he said gravely. "Tell me everything, and don't leave out any details, no matter how trivial."

Harold adjusted himself on the pillow and began with

the holdup. Henry leaned back in his chair, looked at his brother, and listened attentively.

Harold pushed himself away from the table with his good arm and said, "That was a marvelous lunch, ladies."

"It was a very magnificent lunch," emphasized Henry. "My brother has become accustomed to your cooking and doesn't fully appreciate it."

"Thank you," said Abby.

"You still know how to flatter," chided Victoria. "And I like it, so don't stop."

Turning to Brad and Audrey, Henry asked, "Could you take me to Reverend Wesley this afternoon so I can talk to him about Duke?"

"Yes," said Audrey.

"When do you want to leave?" asked Brad.

"Right now is fine," he replied.

"I'll saddle the horses," said Brad.

"While you're gone, I'm going to practice the new hymn for church tomorrow. It's called 'To God Be the Glory.' Fanny Crosby wrote the words and William Doane composed the music. So, have your voices ready to sing after dinner tonight," warned Mrs. Benton.

Reverend Wesley told Henry about his experience with Duke Badger and answered several questions. Henry stood up and said, "Thanks for the information, Reverend. I appreciate you sharing your experience with me."

"You're invited to our Sunday morning service," said Reverend Wesley. "Ten o'clock."

"I'll be there," replied Henry. "Brad and Audrey will make sure of that."

"That's right," agreed Brad.

"I'll be at the sheriff's office about nine o'clock," continued Henry. "That's when Running Bear is due to arrive on the train from St. Louis. I plan to have a little talk with Garth while I'm waiting for Running Bear."

Sunday morning at nine o'clock, Audrey and her uncle stopped in front of the sheriff's office.

"I hear the train whistle," said Audrey. "It must be nine. You can talk to Garth while I take your horse to the depot for Running Bear."

"Good idea," replied Henry, handing Audrey the reins to his horse. "I'll see you shortly."

Audrey clucked Blaze and headed toward the depot. Running Bear had just gotten off the train when Audrey arrived.

"Running Bear, over here, I have a horse for you," called Audrey.

"Miss Benton. What a pleasure to see you with a horse, especially since I have two bags."

"I thought you'd prefer to ride to the sheriff's office," said Audrey.

"How do you know I am going to the sheriff's office? Or should I not ask?" chuckled Running Bear.

"I'll tell you on the way."

Running Bear put one bag behind Audrey and then

mounted Henry's horse with the other bag. In a few minutes, they reached the sheriff's office.

"It is nice to know that you found your father and that he is doing well," said Running Bear as they dismounted.

"You were a good teacher," said Audrey. "We did what you taught us, and we succeeded."

Running Bear smiled and said, "Please introduce me to your uncle, the U. S. Marshal."

"Welcome back to Riverton, Bear," said Sheriff Tate as Running Bear entered the office.

Running Bear set his bags down by the front door. "It's good to be back. Audrey told me that Marshal Benton is here and that he wishes to speak with me."

"That's right; he's in the back talking with Garth."

"I'll take him back," offered Audrey.

Audrey opened the door to the cells; Running Bear followed her. Henry turned to see who had entered.

"Henry Benton, meet Running Bear," said Audrey.

He extended his hand which was quickly engulfed by Running Bear's hand. "Audrey described you quite accurately," said Henry. "Let's go out front and talk."

"I'm goin' ta git you girlie," growled Garth through his bandaged jaw. "No one breaks my jaw an' gits away with it."

Garth reached through the bars of his cell for Audrey. Henry saw him grabbing at her, stepped between them, and ushered Audrey to Sheriff Tate's office.

"Do not threaten the young lady," said Running Bear. "That is not nice. She could have shot you instead of breaking your jaw."

"No Injun can tell me what ta do," mumbled Garth. "I've killed plenty o' Injuns, an' you'll be next."

In an instant, Running Bear grabbed Garth's right arm and pulled him tight against the bars. Garth's bandaged face rammed the cell bars, causing him to gasp in pain. He was helpless and couldn't push away from the bars or even shield his broken jaw because his left arm was pinned at an awkward angle between his body and the bars. With his right hand, Running Bear reached through the bars and grabbed Garth's belt, lifting him off the floor until they were eye-to-eye.

"You are lower than buffalo droppings," hissed Bear. "Be thankful that I am a Christian, or I would kill you now. I have killed white men in battle and have seen them kill my brothers in battle. Those white men were honorable warriors. You are not honorable. You are not a man. You are not a warrior."

Garth's face was white with fear and pain as he said, "Lemme' down; it hurts."

"You have not felt pain. My father and my brothers taught me how to cause pain. If I ever hear of you speaking impolitely to the young lady again, I will find you. I will let you feel the pain that you so richly deserve. Apologize to her for your rude words, or if you wish, I can start your pain now. What do you wish to do?"

"I'm sorry," gasped Garth. "Please lemme' down. I'll apologize t' her."

"Say it now, and say it very loud so that she can hear you," hissed Running Bear.

"I'm sorry young lady," growled Garth as loud as he could through his bandaged jaw. "Please forgive me."

Running Bear slowly returned Garth to the floor and released him. The two prisoners in the adjoining cell watched quietly, their eyes wide in amazement. Garth stumbled back and sank onto his bunk, his face drained of blood, his body weak from pain.

"Thank you," whispered Running Bear. "You are learning how to act like a man."

Running Bear left the jail, gently closing the door behind him.

"We can now talk," said Running Bear.

Henry showed Running Bear his U.S. Marshal's badge. "Bear, I need an excellent tracker. Everyone I've talked to tells me there are three people in the Riverton area with those qualifications, and that you are one of them. I've been assigned the task of bringing in the Badger Gang. Will you help me?"

"When do you wish to start hunting for Duke Badger?" asked Running Bear.

"In about a week," he replied. "I've got to order some equipment and send some telegrams. I also need someplace out of town to use as my headquarters. I can adjust the departure date for you, if you wish."

"Yes, I can help you. I will be ready in one week," said Running Bear.

Audrey looked at the sheriff and said, "How about the old Big Foot Ranch for the headquarters? I'm sure Hank Lacy would let you use it."

"Audrey is right. That would be an excellent location for you," confirmed Bear. "I will introduce you to Mr. Lacy at church."

"We'd better go now," said Audrey noting the clock on the sheriff's wall.

In a few minutes, they arrived at the church. Harold, Victoria, and Brad were already seated and

Abby was playing the piano. Most of the congregation came to shake Harold's hand and congratulate him on his return. The number of the opening hymn was on a large chalkboard on the wall of the church behind Reverend Wesley's pulpit.

Audrey opened the hymnal, grinned, and excitedly gave Brad a gentle poke. "It's 'To God Be the Glory,' the one we practiced last night."

"Fanny Crosby has written hundreds of hymns," said Brad.

"No," corrected Audrey, "she's written over a thousand."

Abby finished playing the prelude, and there was a brief silence as she setup the music for the opening hymn. During this silence, the congregation chatting with each other, returned to their pews, and got ready to sing.

"I'd better get my hymnal and sing, or your mother will make me wish I had," whispered their father.

Abby played the hymn once, and then the congregation started singing. Reverend Wesley's booming bass voice encouraged the congregation not to be bashful, and they weren't. After the opening hymn, a deacon read some verses from the Bible before the reverend rose to speak.

Reverend Wesley strode to the pulpit, grasped the top of it, and slowly gazed out at his congregation. When his eyes reached Harold Benton, he started his sermon. "Harold Benton is with us today. Duke Badger, an utterly despicable monster, lost the battle for Harold's life. Thank you for your prayers."

The congregation was absorbed by the reverend's

sermon. Brad and Audrey were embarrassed by his praise of their bravery, but Running Bear smiled as the reverend briefly described how they had saved their father. When the service was over, Hank Lacy came over, congratulated Brad and Audrey for their courage, and then talked to their father.

"I'll be going, Harold. The folks behind me want to talk to you," said Hank.

"I'll stop by when I'm better," said Harold.

"Mr. Lacy," said Running Bear, "I wish to introduce you to Marshal Henry Benton, Harold's brother."

"Welcome to Riverton, Marshal," said Hank.

"Thanks," said Henry. "I'd like to talk to you about a confidential matter. Can we go outside?"

"Sure, we can go out the back door."

As soon as Hank and Henry left the pew, Harry Acker came over and grabbed Brad and Audrey's hands. "Brad and Audrey to the rescue again," he proclaimed. "I'm glad you found your Pa."

"So are we," said Audrey.

"We had some pretty scary moments," added Brad.

"Especially shooting the wolves as they were about to attack Pa," said Audrey.

Brad and Audrey chatted with Harry, Wilma Sue, and Buck Hodges while they waited for their mother and father. Hank Lacy and Running Bear returned as the last few members of the congregation were leaving the church.

"Let's get together for lunch next Friday, Harold. I'll stop by the stage office a little before noon," said Reverend Wesley as the Bentons left the church.

"I'll be right back, Pa," said Brad running to get the buggy.

"I'll get Blaze and follow you," said Audrey.

"Brad's becoming a man mighty fast," observed Henry. "Audrey's quite a young lady, too."

"Sunday dinner will be ready in about an hour," announced Victoria. "I've already set a place for you, Bear. Please bring your appetite."

"My appetite is very ready after the long train ride. I will be there."

CHAPTER 13
LUTZ HALL IS CAPTURED

Friday, 4 November 1880: Harold Benton was clearing his desk and getting ready for lunch. Reverend Wesley was due to arrive in a few minutes, and he didn't want to make him wait. Harold heard footsteps on the boardwalk, put the letter he was writing in the center desk drawer, and looked expectantly at the door. Although the man was backing into the stage office, Harold could see that the man was taller than the reverend. Harold stood up as the man started turning to face him, the stranger's hand resting on the doorknob.

"What can I do for you?" asked Harold Benton.

"You're dead!" stammered Lutz Hall. He closed the door, and instantly placed his hand on his gun.

"No, I'm very much alive," replied Harold tersely as Lutz came toward him.

Harold and Lutz stopped talking and listened to the footsteps of another man on the boardwalk. Reverend Wesley opened the door and entered the stage office.

"Sell this man a ticket so we can go to lunch," said the reverend, looking at Lutz.

"Reverend Wesley, this is Lutz Hall. He works for Duke Badger," replied Harold.

Lutz tapped his pistol. "Don't make me use this thing. Now both of you; move over there."

Reverend Wesley and Harold started moving back to the wall as Lutz ordered. Harold stumbled and instinctively grasped the reverend's arm to keep from falling. His hand hit something hard inside Reverend Wesley's jacket. As Harold used his hand to steady himself, he realized that the reverend had a pistol inside of his jacket.

"Sorry, Reverend. I'm still a little weak," explained Harold.

"That's okay," answered the reverend. "When facing Goliath, I have strength of David."

"What do ya mean by that, preacher man?" demanded Lutz.

"Ooooohh," groaned Harold Benton as he stumbled to his desk and slumped to the floor.

Lutz stared at Harold lying on the floor and boasted, "You're next preacher man."

"No, you are," replied Reverend Wesley, pointing his Peacemaker at Lutz.

"What the!" exclaimed Lutz.

"Now slowly raise your hands and place them behind your head," ordered the reverend.

"You'd better know how to use that, Preacher," challenged Lutz, moving his hand toward his pistol.

Reverend Wesley squeezed the trigger. The room resounded with the explosion from the reverend's Peacemaker. Lutz's hat whisked off his head and fell to the floor.

"I'm a marksman at thirty paces with this six-shooter," declared the reverend. "You can walk to the sheriff's office or be carried to the undertaker. Please decide by the count of three."

Lutz stared in disbelief at his hat on the floor.

"One!" roared the reverend.

Lutz looked at the Peacemaker aimed at his chest, the smoke curling upward from its barrel.

"Two!"

"I'll walk," squawked Lutz, putting his hands behind his head.

"I'll open the door for you," offered Harold as he got up from the floor.

He opened the door and Lutz slowly walked out with his hands behind his head. Sheriff Tate was running down the street to the stage office carrying a shotgun.

"Anyone hurt?" asked the sheriff.

"No one's hurt," replied Harold. "Reverend Wesley has just captured Lutz Hall, an escaped convict, and a member of the Duke Badger Gang."

"Don't even think about trying anything," warned Hank Lacy, coming out from the alley beside the stage office, his pistol pointing at Lutz.

"We'll give you a cell beside Garth Pugh," said the sheriff as Hank took Lutz's pistol.

Reverend Wesley turned to Harold and said, "Let's have lunch. David Acker always has something special on Friday."

"Sounds mighty good right now; that groan and fall took a lot of energy."

"It was just the diversion I needed to do the Lord's work," said the reverend, putting his pistol back in his shoulder holster.

"I knew you wouldn't need much," agreed Harold.

"Lutz Hall is a tough man," remarked the reverend.

"There's probably a reward for him," predicted Harold.

"Maybe the reward will be large enough to increase the size of the parsonage and build an addition to the church," pondered the reverend as he stroked his chin.

"Are you hinting that your family is going to get larger," questioned Harold.

"I never hint," laughed Reverend Wesley. "It's a fact. We're expecting a new member of the Wesley family in February. I'll announce it this Sunday."

"That's wonderful," exclaimed Harold. "Riverton needs more citizens.

Saturday, 6 November 1880: Marshal Henry Benton poured himself a cup of coffee from the pot on the sheriff's stove. "How's your new prisoner?"

"He doesn't have a broken jaw like Garth," replied the sheriff. "But, he does have a broken spirit."

Henry added a little sugar to his coffee and stirred it. "The $1,000 reward for Lutz goes to the reverend, right?"

"Right," replied the sheriff. "I'm sure he will put it to good use."

"Did Lutz tell you anything?" asked Henry sitting down.

"Nope, he shakes his head and asks himself how he let a preacher get the drop on him."

"That must have been a real shock," acknowledged Henry.

"He received two powerful shocks," said the sheriff. "First, he thought your brother was dead, eaten by the wolves. And second, a no-nonsense Reverend captures him. He's trying to understand a preacher who gives a man the choice of surrendering or going to the undertaker."

"And that's the same preacher who shot his hat off?" chuckled Henry.

"I suppose you'd like to talk with the new prisoner?" queried the sheriff.

"That's why I'm here. I thought I might learn something."

"I'll be taking Garth to see the Doc in a few minutes," said the sheriff. "That would be a good time to talk to Lutz. He'll be the only one in the jail."

"I'll help you with Garth," offered Henry.

The sheriff pulled a pair of handcuffs from his desk drawer and stood up. Henry rose and followed him into the jail.

"Morning Garth," said the sheriff, "it's time to visit Doc Adams."

Garth got up from his bunk and slowly walked the few steps to the bars. Sheriff Tate held out the cuffs. Garth extended his left hand for the sheriff to cuff it. Then he slowly turned around, and the sheriff cuffed the right hand. Sheriff Tate opened the cell door, and Garth sullenly walked out.

Henry waited until the door to the sheriff's office closed and said, "Good morning, Lutz."

Lutz opened his eyes, looked at Henry, and asked. "Who're you?"

"I'm Henry Benton, United States Marshal. I have some questions to ask you. What brings you to Riverton?"

"Jus' passin' through," mumbled Lutz.

"You ride your horse into town and tie it up at the hitching rail in front of the general store. Then you go to the stage office. Were you planning to take the stage to Denver?"

"I got mixed up fer a bit; I thought it was the barbershop." Lutz pulled his hat down over his face and lay back on his bunk.

"Why did Duke Badger send you to Riverton?" asked Henry.

"I told you I was jus' passin' through."

"Then why were you shocked to see Harold Benton alive? You thought Duke's shooting him and leaving him for the wolves had finished him, right?"

Lutz stood up, looked at Henry, and said, "I've heard yer lookin' fer for Duke Badger. All I can tell you is that he's a mean man. No one crosses him an' lives to tell about it. I want ta live t' a ripe old age. Do ya understan'?"

"I understand," replied Henry. "If I hear anything, I can forget who told me. Of course, if I don't hear anything, I can let it be known that someone told me some interesting things about Duke Badger. What would you like me to say when I visit the saloons this afternoon?"

Lutz stared at Henry, anger streaming from his eyes. Henry looked back, his steel blue eyes boring into Lutz. The silence, although brief, seemed like an hour to both men. Lutz's life depended on his remaining silent; and Henry's success hinged on Lutz talking about the Badger Gang.

"I understand'" sighed Lutz, "but don't mention my name. I want ta go back east an' live."

156

"That certainly sounds better than having someone take your coat and boots," conceded Henry. "Why, you might be shot in the shoulder, abandoned in a blizzard miles from the nearest ranch, and then left for the wolves."

Lutz looked at Henry; a cold shiver ran down his back at the thought of facing the same fate that Harold Benton had faced. Lutz looked out his cell window and began talking about Duke. Henry listened intently, and asked a few questions.

"He has about 10 men at his ranch, and a couple o' women," concluded Lutz. "I heard talk 'bout a tunnel. S'posedly he captured some Indians an' forced 'em ta dig a tunnel."

"Can you tell me anything else about the tunnel?" asked Henry.

"I've told ya all I know," explained Lutz. "I never saw it, an Duke never said anythin' 'bout it.

The front door to the sheriff's office opened, and Lutz abruptly stopped talking.

"If you think of anything else, let Sheriff Tate know that you need to see me. I'll be stopping by every few days for the next week or so. And thanks for risking Duke's wrath by slipping some food to my brother. I won't forget your act of kindness."

"I'm not tellin' ya anythin'!" growled Lutz defiantly as Garth was ushered into the jail.

"I can put in a good word for you at the prison if you tell me about Duke," said Henry.

"I'll say it agin', I'm not tellin' ya anythin'."

Sunday morning arrived, and folks came to the Riverton Community Church. Every pew was filled, and folks were standing in the back of the church. The citizens of Riverton had read in Saturday's *Riverton Herald* about Reverend Wesley capturing Lutz Hall. Curiosity may have killed the cat, but in Riverton, it filled the church.

"Ya really packed 'em in, Reverend," said Jake Jackson. "If'n ya keep this up, we'll have ta make the church bigger."

"I held a meeting with the church elders last night," said the reverend. "I'm going to ask that the church and the parsonage be enlarged."

"Enlarge the parsonage?" asked Jake. "Why?"

"Abby's starting the opening hymn," replied the reverend. "I'll tell you later."

Reverend Wesley walked to the front of the church, singing his heart out to the Lord. Jake Jackson scratched his head about what the reverend had said. At the end of the service, Reverend Wesley made his usual announcements. Today, he told the congregation that his family would welcome an additional member in February. Not one to let folks worry about raising money for the building fund, he held up a yellow sheet of paper.

"I received a telegram from Marshal Strong yesterday. There is a thousand-dollar reward for the capture of Lutz Hall. That reward will buy the materials for the addition to the parsonage and enlarging the church." There was a murmur of approval from the congregation at this revelation.

Reverend Wesley continued. "Just before the service, the elders met and appointed Jake Jackson the Building Coordinator. He'll draw up the plans for their approval, schedule the delivery of supplies, and determine the day of the church raising. Abby, our closing hymn please."

After the service, everyone wanted to shake the reverend's hand. Not only did he capture Lutz Hall, but he also got the funds to pay for enlarging the parsonage and the church.

"Harold," said Sheriff Tate. "I'll be hiring a new deputy tomorrow morning. I want Garth Pugh and Lutz Hall under guard 24 hours a day."

"I'm glad to hear that," replied Harold. "They're both dangerous men."

"Duke's not afraid of anything, except bears," said Audrey. "He'll break them out if he finds out they're in Riverton's jail."

"The Lord will take care of that evil monster," said Victoria. "Just make sure those two are well guarded."

"They will be," confirmed the sheriff. "They'll be under constant guard."

"You're not taking any chances," observed Brad.

"Duke will eventually find out about Garth and Lutz going back to prison. He'll also find out about your father," the sheriff grinned, "but I'm not going to make it easy for him."

"Thank you, Sheriff," said Abby. "I don't want him and his henchman in this town."

"Please excuse me," said the sheriff. "I've got to go. I'll see you Monday, Harold. I've got to check on my prisoners."

"And my two Pinkertons have overdue homework

to finish," said Abby putting her arms around Brad and Audrey.

"I'll get the buggy," said Brad.

"I'll get our horses," added Audrey.

Brad brought the buggy to the front of the church where Harold, Abby, and Victoria were waiting for him. He helped Victoria and his mother into the buggy. Harold climbed in, took the reins, gave a gentle slap, and they headed for home.

"Brad," said Audrey. "Let's not race home. I'll give you the biggest piece of pie."

"It's a deal," said Brad. "Besides, Nana has been feeding me constantly since we brought Pa back. She says I have to get some meat back on my bones."

Brad and Audrey mounted their horses, gave them a soft cluck, and headed home at a walk.

ADDENDUM
FANNY CROSBY AND "TO
GOD BE THE GLORY"

Fanny Crosby was one of the shapers of American culture; she met and influenced the political, religious, and business leaders of her lifetime. Her gift for poetry helped to deeply embed Christianity in the history and culture of the United States.

Fanny Crosby wrote the text of the hymn, "Praise for Redemption," later retitled, "To God Be the Glory," in 1872 or 1873, and William Doane, a friend and musician, set it to music.

An associate of Doane, Ira Sankey, included the hymn in his *Sacred Songs and Solos* hymnal published in England in 1874, and it is still used there today.

Sankey was the music director for the evangelist, Dwight L. Moody, who founded the Moody Bible Institute in Chicago. Returning to the United States from England, Sankey, Doane, and Robert Lowry included this hymn in their 1875 Sunday school collection, *Brightest and Best.*

Three quarters of a century later, a religious leader from London recommended that "To God Be the Glory" be included in a songbook Cliff Barrows (music director for Billy Graham) was compiling for use in Graham's 1952 Greater London Crusade. Although Cliff Barrows didn't know the hymn, he did include it, and it proved to be very popular. Two years later, Barrows successfully re-introduced it to America in Billy Graham's 1954 Nashville Crusade. Its popularity continues in today's American hymnals.

Fanny Crosby was born on March 24, 1820, in South East, Putnam County, New York. At the age of six weeks, she became quite ill. The people treating her "poulticed" her eyes, but their ineptness destroyed her sight. A poultice is a hot pack of wet herbs that is held against the afflicted area; it was a common treatment for a variety of illnesses of that era. At fifteen, Fanny entered the New York State Institution for the Blind as a student. She remained at the institution for twelve years as a teacher. In 1858, she married Alexander Van Alstyne, whom she had met when they were both students.

Fanny liked poetry, studied the great poets, and wrote poetry. The Institution took its students to schools and churches to show what the blind could do. The poems Fanny recited included many of her own.

When President John Tyler (1840-45) visited the Institution, Fanny recited some of her poetry for him. She also established a close rapport with presidents Martin Van Buren (1837-41), William Henry Harrison (1841), James Polk (1845-49), and Grover Cleveland (1885-89 and 1893-97).

When William Bradbury, a hymnist, asked Fanny to write a hymn for him, she gave him the text for her first hymn, "We Are Going, We Are Going" three days after his request. From that date forward, she knew that her life's work was to be a hymn writer. Bradbury was a composer, piano manufacturer, and music publisher who also served as organist and choir director at several Baptist churches in New York City.

Fanny departed the New York State Institution for the Blind in the 1850s when she started collaborating with George Root, who had been her music teacher at the Institution. Root was a prolific American composer, best known for "The Battle Cry of Freedom."

Fanny's first hymn to receive wide acceptance was "Pass Me Not, O Gentle Savior," which she wrote in 1868. William Doane, one of her life-long hymn partners, wrote the music for this and 1,000 other texts given to him by Fanny. Doane was a manufacturer of woodworking equipment and president of a number of firms. He held patents for 70 inventions and compiled Sunday school hymnals with Robert Lowry as well as *The Baptist Hymnal* of 1883.

In 1869, Fanny wrote the text for "Praise Him! Praise Him!" set to music by Chester Allen. She wrote "Blessed Assurance" in 1873, and her friend Phoebe Palmer Knapp wrote the music. Phoebe was the wife of Joseph Knapp, founder of the Metropolitan Life Insurance Company.

Some other well-known works by Fanny include

"Tell Me the Story of Jesus," "Saved by Grace," and "My Savior First of All." She wrote the text for over 8,000 hymns.

Fanny Crosby died on February 12, 1915 in Bridgeport, Connecticut. Reverend George Brown of Fanny's church, the First Methodist Episcopal

Church of Bridgeport, and the minister of the People's Presbyterian Church, conducted her funeral which was attended by all the ministers of Bridgeport, many from the surrounding area, and a large number from many denominations in other cities.

ADDENDUM
JULES VERNE AND *20,000 LEAGUES UNDER THE SEA*

Jules Verne was born on February 8, 1828, in Nantes, France. Nantes is a manufacturing and commercial city on the Loire River in northwest France, about 30 miles inland from the Bay of Biscay. In his mid-teens, he apprenticed as a law clerk in his father's legal practice. After apprenticing, he went to Paris in 1847 to complete his law studies at the prestigious Faculty of Law. While a student in Paris, he met the well-known author and playwright Alexander Dumas. Dumas is the author of *The Count of Monte Cristo* and *The Three Musketeers*. Verne was fascinated with the theater and spent many hours with Dumas. He actively pursued his literary interest while studying law. Jules' first successful play, *The Broken Straws*, was produced in 1850. In the mid-1850s, after completing his law studies, he became a stockbroker but continued writing plays and stories.

His first novel, *Five Weeks in a Balloon*, was published in 1863, followed by *Voyage to the Center of the Earth* in 1864. In 1865, he received a letter from a Romantic novelist, George Sand, the pen name for the wife of the composer/pianist, Frederick Chopin. Her publisher, Pierre Hetzel, was the same one used by Jules Verne.

She urged Jules to write a book about an underwater sea voyage. Four years later, *20,000 Leagues Under the Sea* was published in softcover. It was released in two parts; part one in October 1869, and part two in June 1870. The Franco-Prussian War delayed publication of the hardcover edition until the fall of 1871. The official 1871 first edition, in French, of course, was beautifully bound in red and gold cloth. It featured two maps and over a hundred black and white illustrations.

Due to the tremendous success of Verne's previous book, *Around the World in Eighty Days*, the English publisher for his works, Sampson, Low, Marston, & Co. needed the English translation as soon as possible. They hired an Oxford cleric, Reverend Louis Mercier, to translate the book. Unfortunately, due to the rush to publish an English version, the translation had many errors and omitted about twenty-five percent of the original French edition. Reverend Mercier's translation is the edition familiar to most of the English speaking world. Future versions of *20,000 Leagues Under the Sea* continued and added more errors and omissions of Mercier's first translation.

Verne continued writing science fiction novels, averaging about one book a year, until his death in Amiens, France on March 24, 1905.

In 1989, Walter J. Miller and Frederick P. Walter collaborated to produce a new and accurate English translation of *20,000 Leagues Under the Sea.* The result was the definitive, unabridged edition based on the original French texts. The Naval Institute Press, Annapolis, Maryland, published this highly accurate edition in 1993.

Walter J. Miller and Frederick P. Walter researched and produced an excellent English translation. Unique terms and background information are provided via footnotes at the bottom of each page. If an accurate and complete English version of Jules Verne's famous novel is desired, this is the book to read.

BRAD AND AUDREY HELP SET A TRAP TO CAPTURE AN ARSONIST.

FOR AN EXCERPT, TURN THE PAGE.

CHAPTER 1
FIRE!

Friday, 19 November 1880: Audrey opened her eyes and slowly sat up. She brushed the hay off her coat and looked around the dark barn. Something wasn't right. "Brad, wake up," she said.

"I'm awake," he said, reaching down from the top bunk to touch his sister's shoulder. "What is it?"

"I think I smell smoke."

"Smoke?" questioned her brother, sitting up and sniffing the air. "I smell it, too."

Both of them threw off their blankets and quickly put on their boots. Blaze and Ebony nickered and pawed the floor of the barn.

Brad opened the tack room door and yelled, "Fire! The house is on fire!"

Falling snow muffled the sound of breaking glass as Vasya Petrov smashed a chair through the bedroom window of his burning house. Brad and Audrey ran through the blizzard toward the blaze. Flames engulfed the front of the house and were racing across the roof by the time Brad and Audrey reached the bedroom window.

"Help Olga!" screamed Vasya through the broken window. Smoke snaked around Olga, then shot upward once outside as she struggled to climb out.

Brad and Audrey helped Olga through the broken window. As soon as Vasya saw that his wife was free, he dove headfirst through the window into the snow. His long johns were smoking, as was his hair. Flames pursued him out the window, like evil hands trying to pull him back into the inferno from which he had just escaped.

"Your hair!" shouted Audrey. Releasing Olga, she threw herself on Vasya's smoldering head, pushing it into the snow.

Brad cupped his hands, scooped a mound of wet snow, and pushed it under Audrey onto Vasya's still smoldering hair.

"Vasya!" screamed his wife. "Vasya!"

"I not hurt," assured Vasya, rising to his hands and knees.

"We've got to get away from the house," said Brad as windblown firebrands swirled around them, hissing as they fell into the snow. "Thank God the wind isn't blowing the fire toward the barn."

Vasya stood up and tenderly wrapped his arms around his wife.

"Vasya, we almost die," whimpered his shivering wife, the snow swirling around her bare feet.

"Mr. Petrov," urged Brad, "let's go to the barn. It will shelter us from the blizzard."

Vasya carried his wife to the barn. Audrey brought a couple of empty feed bags and wrapped them around Olga's feet. Brad picked up an old horse blanket from a peg on the tack room wall and wrapped it around Olga's shivering body.

"Thank you," said Olga. "My shoes in house with clothes."

The four of them stood in the tack room doorway watching flames devour the house. Their faces flushed from the heat of the fire as their backs shivered from the cold wind whipping around them. Tears streamed down the Petrovs' faces as the flames slowly subsided.

"Olga," consoled Vasya, his arms around his wife, "we live. We not die in fire."

"Is winter now," said Olga. "We no have money. We no have food. We not live long."

"You won't die," insisted Audrey.

"We'll go to Bevins' general store first thing in the morning," said Brad. "We'll get you some shoes and clothes."

"Reverend Wesley will help too," added Audrey. "The church will help you."

"You not understand," said Olga. "Church not help. You see."

The four of them gazed at the burning embers of the house through the subsiding blizzard. A sudden gust of wind blew a clump of snow from a tree onto the smoldering remains. Little puffs of steam accompanied the sizzle of melting snow.

Brad lit the tack room lantern, and said, "Audrey, when I put the horses in the barn last night, I think saw a jacket. Help me take a look for it."

They searched around the barn and found the jacket Brad had seen earlier, as well as a pair of old boots.

"Here, these should help," offered Brad, handing them to Vasya.

"Thank you." Vasya put on the jacket. "Barn jacket. Barn boots. I wear when work in barn."

"The tack room will provide shelter until morning," said Brad. "Then we can go into Riverton."

"They need clothes or blankets," reminded Audrey.

"Horse blankets," sniffed Brad, picking one up. "They may smell like a horse, but they'll at least keep you warm tonight."

Audrey held the lantern as her brother picked up Blaze and Ebony's saddle blankets. Returning to the tack room, Brad put the blankets on the bunk for the Petrovs.

"Brad and I have our long underwear and coats," Audrey assured Vasya. "We'll sleep in the hay. You and Mrs. Petrov can share the bunk in the tack room. Mrs. Petrov, the burlap bags should help keep your feet warm. While you're getting settled, Brad and I will fill a couple of empty feed bags with hay to cover you. That with the blankets should keep you warm until morning."

When Brad and Audrey returned with the hay-stuffed feed bags, the Petrovs settled into the bunk. Vasya wrapped his arms around his wife and they huddled together beneath the blankets. Olga sobbed as Brad covered them with the bags of hay. Brad and Audrey quietly left the tack room as Vasya soothed his wife in their native Russian language.

"Brad," whispered Audrey, "it's terrible. Their house is gone; they have nothing."

"True," agreed Brad, "but we'll take them to the general store first thing tomorrow morning. We've got to get them some clothes as soon as possible. Between

Mr. Bevins and Reverend Wesley, we'll get the Petrovs through the winter. Right now, we've got to get ourselves settled for the night."

Audrey held the lantern while Brad got their saddles and put them in the hay bin. Together, they leveled the hay in front of their saddles and spread a few empty feed bags on top of the hay.

"It's fortunate that Vasya had these empty feed bags," said Brad as he filled one with hay.

"They'll help keep us warm tonight," said Audrey. "A bag of hay isn't as good as a blanket, but with our long underwear, we'll be okay."

When they had stuffed four bags with hay, Audrey laid down and pulled two of the bags on top of her. Brad blew out the lantern and hung it on a large peg. When his eyes adjusted to the dark, he crept to his new bed. Feeling for his saddle, he laid down and covered himself with the other bags of hay.

"Good night, Audrey," said Brad, tugging up his coat collar.

"Good night, Brad," replied his sister.

Saturday, 20 November 1880: The rooster's crow woke Brad. He reached over and touched his sister, "It's time to get up, Audrey."

"Brad," she muttered groggily, "did I hear a rooster?"

"Yes," he said. "It's the Petrovs' rooster."

The fire, the Petrovs, the barn, and the blizzard abruptly came to the forefront of Audrey's thoughts. As she slowly sat up, she saw that Brad was brushing hay off his clothes.

"I hear the Petrovs stirring," said Brad. "As soon as they're up, I can get our blankets to saddle the horses."

"That isn't going to be very long," said Audrey. "I can hear his boots on the floor now."

"Morning," greeted Vasya, coming out of the tack room. "I thank you for saving our lives."

"Yes," said Olga. "Thank you. We have no house, but we have barn, livestock."

"I'm glad we were here to help," said Brad.

"Now, we need to get you some clothes," said Audrey.

"You right. We hitch horse to wagon for trip to town," said Vasya, his arm around his wife.

"I'll get the harness while you get your horse," Brad told Vasya.

Several minutes later, the Petrovs' horse was harnessed and hitched to the wagon. Brad saddled Blaze and Ebony while Audrey and Vasya put the bags of hay on the floor and seat of the wagon to help keep the Petrovs warm.

"We're ready," said his sister, standing in the barn doorway.

Brad led Ebony and Blaze out of the barn while Vasya picked up his wife and carried her through the snow to the wagon. Shivering from the cold, she clutched the blanket tightly around herself as she settled down into the bag of hay. Vasya climbed into the wagon seat, and Audrey wrapped a second blanket around Olga's legs and feet, topping the blanket with another bag of hay.

"We go," announced Vasya, slapping the reins on the back of the horse.

Before mounting their horses, Brad and Audrey

watched the wagon move past the snow-covered ashes of the house.

"This is terrible," Audrey said, gently nudging Blaze to a slow trot. "Their house, their clothes, their furniture, all of it is gone." She paused for a moment and then continued, "They lost everything except the barn and the livestock."

"They even lost the new blankets and supplies that we delivered for Mr. Bevins yesterday," said Brad.

"But not the long johns," said Audrey. "Vasya wore them last night, or he wouldn't even have had them today."

"And Olga wouldn't have her old blankets that she gave us when the blizzard forced us to sleep in their barn last night, either," added Brad.

The ride to Riverton went swiftly with the morning sun's warmth melting the snow on the road. The wagon and horses sloshed their way down Riverton's Main Street.

Just after Mr. Bevins opened the general store, Vasya parked his wagon in front and helped his wife down. Brad opened the door for the Petrovs who hurried into the warmth of the store.

"Come with me to the stove, Mr. Petrov," invited Audrey. "You're freezing."

"I not want to die," said Olga as her husband put his arms around her and walked with her to the stove.

"We not die," said Vasya assuringly. "We live. We still have barn."

Tears streamed down Olga Petrov's face. Her fearful eyes darted to Mr. Bevins.

"Mrs. Petrov," exclaimed Mr. Bevins. "What's wrong? Why should you die?"

"Our house burn last night; we now live in barn."

"That's terrible," replied Mr. Bevins. "Were you able to save anything?"

"We save ourselves," recounted Vasya. "Fire very fast; kitchen all flames. We leave through window."

"You have no shoes," said Mr. Bevins, staring at Olga's burlap-wrapped feet. Looking more closely, he saw that only a blanket covered her flannel nightdress. Vasya was clad a little better with a pair of old boots and his barn jacket covering the top of his long underwear. Pink scalp showed where his hair had been singed.

"I'll get you some clothes and blankets," declared Mr. Bevins. "First, however, how about some hot coffee and a sandwich?"

"Thank you," said Olga, smiling for the first time since the fire.

Mr. Bevins went to the stove, poured two cups of coffee, and handed them to the Petrovs. Then he reached under the counter and brought out a flour sack with some sandwiches and apples.

"Roast beef sandwiches," he said, handing them to the Petrovs.

"But that your lunch," protested Vasya.

"True, but now it is your breakfast," Mr. Bevins insisted. "My wife and daughter will be arriving with their lunches later this morning. I'll share with them; my wife always packs too much food anyway. Please, eat and enjoy."

He turned away from the Petrovs, looked at Audrey and Brad, and murmured, "Audrey, please ask Sheriff

Tate to come right away. Brad, see if Reverend Wesley can come, too.”

“Yes, sir,” said Audrey, heading to the door.

“I’ll take Ebony,” said Brad. “The reverend and I can ride double on the way back.”

Minutes later, Audrey burst into the sheriff’s office only to find it empty. She had just decided to head back out when the door behind her opened, startling her.

“Audrey, I saw you rush in. What can I do for you?”

“The Petrovs’ home burned down last night,” she told the sheriff. “They’re at the general store now. Mr. Bevins asked me to bring you right away.”

“Let’s go then,” he said, holding the door open for her.

While Audrey and Sheriff Tate were heading to the general store, Brad had dismounted from Ebony and was knocking on Reverend Wesley’s door.

“Why, Brad,” welcomed Mrs. Wesley, “what can we do for you this fine morning?”

“I came for the reverend; is he in?” asked Brad.

“He sure is,” hollered Reverend Wesley, coming out of the kitchen. “I trust there hasn’t been another stage holdup.”

Reverend Wesley was referring to a recent stagecoach holdup by the Badger Gang. Brad, Audrey, and their father had been passengers on that stagecoach.

“No holdup, but there was a fire,” responded Brad. “The Petrovs’ home burned down last night. They’re at the general store right now, and Mr. Bevins is supplying them with some clothes and blankets. He asked me to come get you.”

“Sounds like the church can help them. Let me grab my coat, and I’ll be right with you.”

"I brought Ebony," said Brad. "We can ride double to the general store."

Brad mounted Ebony and then took his foot out of the left stirrup. The reverend used the empty stirrup and mounted behind Brad. Brad gently pulled the reins to the left and clucked to his horse. They rode down the street toward the general store, arriving a few minutes after Audrey and Sheriff Tate.

"Morning, Reverend," nodded the sheriff.

"Morning, Richard," replied the reverend. "Let's go see what we can do to help."

"Brad," said the sheriff, "please go to the livery and bring my horse. Bring the reverend's horse, too. I think we're going to take a ride out to the Petrovs'."

When they entered the general store, they saw Mr. Bevins talking to the Petrovs. Reverend Wesley noticed the burlap bags wrapped around Mrs. Petrov's feet and the long johns under her husband's barn jacket.

"Brad said your home burned down last night," said Reverend Wesley. "It must have been bad. Can you tell me about it?"

"It happen fast," recalled Vasya. "Fire everywhere. We climb out window."

"A fire usually gives you more time than that, but not always," remarked the sheriff. "Did you hear anything just before the fire?"

"I hear glass break, but Vasya no hear," said Olga.

"Breaking glass," noted the sheriff thoughtfully. "Anything else unusual? Did you smell anything?"

"Maybe kerosene, I not sure," said Olga.

"Brad, Audrey, did you hear anything unusual?" Sheriff Tate inquired.

"Something woke me up, but I don't know what," answered Audrey. "After I woke up, I smelled smoke, and then heard the tinkle of glass as Mr. Petrov broke the bedroom window so they could escape the fire."

"Let's ride out to your place," the sheriff told the Petrovs. "I'd like to have a look around."

"I not want to make trouble," appealed Vasya. "You stay. No need to come."

"It's my job, and it's no trouble," the sheriff assured him.

"Vasya, you can borrow my horse and ride out with the sheriff," said the reverend. "I'll get some additional supplies and follow in the wagon with your wife."

"We have no money for supplies," protested Vasya, buttoning his new overalls.

"That may be true," said the reverend as he handed a new jacket to Vasya, "but when someone around here experiences a tragedy, like your fire, folks help each other. Just like you did in the search for Harold Benton, we're here for you."

Outside the general store, Brad looped the reins of the three horses over the hitching rail. Audrey was waiting for him at the door.

"What did the sheriff say?" asked Brad, stopping outside the store to confer with his sister.

"Not much. He's going to ride out with Vasya and look at what's left of their house. Reverend Wesley is going later in the wagon with Olga and some more supplies. I'll be helping them load the wagon. Let's go inside."

"I see you're back," said the sheriff as Brad closed the door. "Are the horses outside?"

"Yes, sir."

Reverend Wesley quickly strode across the store to Sheriff Tate and Vasya. "Vasya, my horse is outside. Why don't you take it and go with the sheriff? I'll follow with your wagon."

Vasya started to object, but Sheriff Tate interrupted him. "Come with me, Vasya. We need to leave now."

Sheriff Tate put his hand on Vasya's shoulder as they departed. Brad and Audrey watched them mount up and start down the street at a slow trot.

"Brad," called Mr. Bevins, "please go over to the hotel and give this note to Mr. Acker. Wait for his reply, and then bring it back to me. Audrey, will you please help Mrs. Petrov select the right pair of shoes while I help my other customers?"

Brad slid the note into his pocket and hurried down the boardwalk. When he reached the hotel, he crossed the lobby, stopped in front of the door marked PRIVATE, and knocked twice.

"Who is it?" inquired Mr. Acker.

"Brad Benton, sir; I have a note from Mr. Bevins."

"Come on in, Brad."

David Acker was sitting behind a large mahogany desk that held an inkwell, a ledger, and a kerosene lamp. The bright sun was shining through the window onto a rather large sheet of white parchment that Mr. Acker was examining intently.

"I was just checking the hotel's Thanksgiving menu," he said as he walked around the desk to greet Brad.

"Mr. Bevins asked me to bring you this note."

"Thank you," said Mr. Acker, reaching for the piece of paper.

He stroked his chin thoughtfully as he read. "Brad, have a seat."

Brad sat down as Mr. Acker pulled a thick decorative rope hanging from the wall and returned to his desk. He opened a drawer and withdrew another ledger. He had just lifted the ledger's cover when the side door to his office opened.

"Yes, Mr. Acker?" inquired a waitress.

"Sally, the Petrovs' house burned down last night. They lost everything and spent the night in their barn. I'd like you to pack a box with some food: several loaves of bread, some meat, rolls, a pie, whatever you can quickly put together that doesn't require cooking. Take the box to the front desk, and Brad will stop by in about ten minutes to pick it up."

"I'll start on it right away," she said, turning to leave. "Brad's name will be on the box when he comes to get it."

"Thanks, Sally. I'll have the reply for Mr. Bevins in a minute, Brad," said Mr. Acker.

He dipped his pen in the inkwell and wrote a brief note. When he finished, he rolled a blotter over the paper. He repeated the process after he wrote a check to go with the note. He opened another drawer to retrieve an envelope and inserted them into it.

"This is the reply for Mark. I've included a check to Bevins' General Store. I know he didn't ask for it, but tell him a box of food will be ready before the reverend arrives with the wagon. And Brad," added Mr. Acker, his eyes twinkling as a smile spread across his face.

"Yes, sir?" said Brad expectantly.

"Thanks for bringing the note. You've been a big

help. Now hurry back to the general store, and say hello to Reverend Wesley for me. Please come back to get the box afterward."

Brad took the envelope and left the hotel. He thought to himself, *I've never seen Mr. Acker at church, yet he's always friendly with Reverend Wesley. I wonder why he doesn't come to church."*

Brad entered the general store and halted briefly to let his eyes adjust to the dimness of the unlit store. Mr. Bevins was behind the counter, and his daughter, Wilma Sue, was across the store helping a woman select some cloth. Brad quickly walked up to Mr. Bevins and gave him the envelope.

"That was pretty fast," remarked Mr. Bevins.

"Brad," said Reverend Wesley, coming out of the back room, "will you help me load this box into the wagon?"

"Yes, sir."

Brad picked up one end of the box, the reverend the other, and they carried it across the boardwalk, lifting it up and onto the back of the wagon.

"Reverend, Mr. Acker said to say hello. He said you didn't ask for it, but he's preparing a box of food for the Petrovs. It will be at the front desk with my name on it."

"That's a very kind thing for him to do. Can you come with us to the hotel? If I know David, I'll need your help with that box, too. It will be a large one."

"Of course," replied Brad. "I'll help you at the hotel while Audrey gets the supplies Nana wanted."

"Olga," called Reverend Wesley, "Are you ready?"

"Yes, Reverend, I ready."

Reverend Wesley and Brad helped Olga climb up to

the wagon seat. Once they were all in, the reverend gently slapped the reins and headed to the hotel. When they arrived, Brad jumped down and went to the front desk.

Moments later he returned to the wagon. "You were right, Reverend, it is a big box. I'll need your help."

"David is a generous man," replied the reverend, climbing down from the wagon. "Let's get that box loaded. There's a lot to do today."

The two of them heaved the box onto the back of the wagon. It was filled with several loaves of bread, some cheese, apples, a pie, and a cloth sack of roast beef.

"There's even a butcher knife, cups, plates, spoons, and forks," observed Brad.

"That's David," said the reverend, climbing back into the wagon. "Thanks for your help, Brad. I'll see you at church tomorrow." The reverend gently slapped the reins, and the wagon lurched forward. Brad looked intently at the wagon as it disappeared past the curve on the snowy street. When he could no longer see it, he started back to the general store. As he entered, his sister turned from the counter, a cloth sack in her hand.

"I've got everything on Nana's list," she said. "Let's go home; I'm ready for breakfast."

Brad looked at her for a moment before answering. "Uh, right, let's go home."

They mounted their horses and started down the street. Audrey looked at her brother as they rode out of town; he stared ahead, oblivious to his surroundings.

"Brad." He didn't respond, but continued riding, deep in thought. "Brad," said Audrey again, this time reaching over and gently poking him in the ribs.

184

"What?" jerked Brad, glancing at his sister.

"What are you thinking about? Did something happen at the hotel?"

"No, I was just thinking about Reverend Wesley and Mr. Acker."

"Well," prodded Audrey, "what about them?"

"Mr. Acker doesn't come to church. Mr. Bevins writes him a note, and Mr. Acker writes a check to the general store." Brad paused, took a deep breath, and continued. "Mr. Acker also gives a big box of food to the Petrovs and asks me to say hello to Reverend Wesley. When I tell the reverend about the box of food, he says it'll be a big box and asks me to come help him load it into the wagon. He acts like he's a close friend of Mr. Acker."

"So?"

"Well, it was a big box. It was a big wooden crate heaped with food and kitchen supplies. I don't understand."

"Don't understand what?"

"Why he does that for total strangers. He doesn't come to church, but he and the reverend act like they're old friends. It just doesn't make sense."

"I see what you mean," Audrey said as they dismounted and led their horses into the barn. "But helping people in need is part of being a Christian."

"Yes, but so is going to church."

"Yes, it is."

"Do you know something about Mr. Acker that I don't know?" asked Brad.

"I don't think so. Maybe we'll learn more in church tomorrow. We can ask Jake Jackson, if he's not too busy. He seems to know just about everything about everyone in Riverton.”

“Good idea,” said Brad. “But first, let’s eat breakfast and tell Ma and Nana about the fire.”

OTHER TITLES BY THIS AUTHOR

THE BIGFOOT GANG

CAPTIVE

FIERY BLIZZARD

ABOUT THE AUTHOR

Born and raised in the West, Smith grew up where many farmers still used horses to plow their fields. Steam engines were the norm for railroads, and a diesel locomotive was quite an event. He's now caught up with modern civilization.

After serving in the U. S. Air Force, he later worked as a teacher, professional musician, and federal employee. He has now settled down and lives in Virginia. You can find out more about him at www.edgsmith.com.

CONNECT WITH THE AUTHOR

Website:
www.edgsmith.com

Social Media:
www.facebook.com/edgsmith

ACKNOWLEDGEMENTS:

Many thanks to Liza Potter for enhancing clarity, editing for all that grammar stuff, and partnering with me to bring the Benton Series to fruition. And to Liza's daughter, Lauren, for the young adult assessment. Kathryn Boudreau, and her dog Daisy, for taking photos and providing encouragement. A special atta-girl for Susie Nunez's special skills in making the liner comments {jacket items (author bio, about paragraph) cover description} come alive.

9 781732 875005